## "I HEARD YOU'VE BEEN
## LOOKING FOR ME."

The drunk rover snickered and added, "So I thought I'd come looking for you and save you the trouble, you son of a bitch!"

Longarm just smiled as he quietly replied, "I'm going to let that pass this time, Mr. Fuller, because I fear we've both been victims of a big fibber. I have no call to be after you and you've never done me wrong, assuming I overlook that rude remark about my possible ancestry."

"You don't feel so brave now that we're face-to-face, eh?" asked Simon Fuller owlishly.

Longarm didn't answer.

"I'm saying here and now I don't think you have the sand in your craw for a fair fight with any man!"

Longarm went on smiling.

Then Simon Fuller slapped leather, and hell erupted.

**TABOR EVANS**

# LONGARM

### AND THE CURSED CORPSE

**J**

**JOVE BOOKS, NEW YORK**

LONGARM AND THE CURSED CORPSE

A Jove Book / published by arrangement with
the author

PRINTING HISTORY
Jove edition / June 1999

All rights reserved.
Copyright © 1999 by Penguin Putnam Inc.
This book may not be reproduced in whole or part,
by mimeograph or any other means, without permission.
For information address: The Berkley Publishing Group,
a division of Penguin Putnam Inc.,
375 Hudson Street, New York, New York 10014.

The Penguin Putnam Inc. World Wide Web site address is
http://www.penguinputnam.com

ISBN: 0-515-12519-9

A JOVE BOOK®
Jove Books are published by The Berkley Publishing Group,
a division of Penguin Putnam Inc.,
375 Hudson Street, New York, New York 10014.
JOVE and the "J" design
are trademarks belonging to Penguin Putnam Inc.

PRINTED IN THE UNITED STATES OF AMERICA

10  9  8  7  6  5  4  3  2  1

# LONGARM

## AND THE
## CURSED CORPSE

# Chapter 1

There was more than one way to skin a cat or tote a gun. U.S. Deputy Marshal Custis Long of the Denver District carried his double-action Colt .44-40 high and cross-draw, because that offered him a handy grab for his gun-grips whether seated or standing, mounted or on foot. The man who was out to kill him that morning had his own Schofield .45-28 in an underslung tied-down side-draw rig, because that offered a marginally faster draw when and if a man got to pick the time and place for a face-to-face on foot.

The lean and hungry-looking individual lurking out front of the Overland Terminal near Tremont and Colfax wasn't there for such a fair fight, of course. He figured to be paid the same bounty or hung by the same neck until dead no matter *how* he blew away the federal lawman, and they said that Longarm, as he was better known to friend and foe alike, could eat cucumbers and perform other wonders with the .44-40 he toted under that tobacco-tweed frock coat. So the man planning to kill him on his way to work at the nearby Federal Building pretended to be craning for some sign of the Julesburg stage as his intended target ambled along the red-sandstone sidewalk of the natural shortcut formed by the triangle of Colfax, Tremont, and Denver's Broadway.

Longarm didn't care whether the Julesburg stage was running early, late, or not at all that morning. The coming of the Iron Horse had only left a few short-line coaching outfits serving the mile-high capital of Colorado, and Longarm was more worried about covering the next few city blocks in his low-heeled cavalry boots before the clock struck nine. He hadn't made it to the office on time in recent memory. But he knew his boss, Marshal Billy Vail, usually showed up before seven, and he hated to see a grown man cry.

So Longarm barely glanced at the cluster of men gathered out front of the Terminal across from the Tremont House Hotel as he legged it past them in the pleasantly crisp breezes of a sunny spring morning. When a man who'd been packing a badge six or eight years thought about it, he figured he had to have made some enemies along the way. But if a lawman thought about it too much, he could get to spooking at shadows and shooting the wrong gents, like poor old James Butler Hickok just before he got to drinking too much. It seemed just as safe to assume nobody was out to gun you unless you saw some son of a bitch go for a gun. And hence, Longarm never saw the one treacherous stranger slap leather until he'd strode on by and it was way too late—or it would have been if things had gone as originally planned that crisp spring morning.

Longarm's first intimation that anything unusual was taking place came in the form of a ten-gauge shotgun blast so close to his spine that he tried to leap out of his boots, and came down to find bits and pieces of bloody hide and hair raining down all around as he dove for the low soggy shelter of a curbside watering trough, pivoted on one heel, and got his own gun out.

The center of his view was occupied by a thinning cloud of gun smoke and the looming outline of a big burly cuss with a sawed-off Double Greener and a hat that looked big enough for a modest Indian family to live in. A leaner individual sprawled at his feet near a smaller Stetson and a Schofield .45-28. Nobody else was in sight at the moment, although the trill of a distant police whistle rent the sudden stillness out front of the Overland Terminal.

Seeing the only other living soul in sight had the twin muzzles of that ten-gauge pointed politely, Longarm gingerly rose to his own considerable height with his .44-40 aimed straight down, and called out in a conversational tone, "Howdy. How come you just now gunned that old boy on the walk? I ain't asking out of idle curiosity. I'm the law. I'd be U.S. Deputy Marshal Custis Long, working out of that big federal building on the far side of the Parthenon Saloon."

The stranger replied in as casual a tone, "I've heard tell of you, Longarm. Reckon this cuss must have too. He was fixing to gun you in the back when I stopped him just now. I'd be Luke Cahill out of Big D, and you may have heard of me as the Caddo Kid."

To which Longarm honestly replied, "Can't say I have, no offense. I fail to see just why anyone might want to describe you as either a Caddo or a kid. I hope you won't take this observation as unkind, but if I had to describe you for a warrant, I'd say you looked sort of Irish and had to be pushing thirty or more. What's the story on this other gent wearing trail duds and a Texas hat?"

Cahill shrugged and replied, "Never seen him before. I figured you were the one who knew him. He wasn't staring hard at *my* back when he drew that cavalry pistol just now. Don't you ever thank a man for passing the salt either? I just now saved your life, you rude cuss!"

Longarm neither put his revolver away nor aimed it at anyone as he stared soberly at the total stranger oozing on the red-sandstone walk between them. Then he grudgingly decided, "Well, I'd likely be just as dead if the two of you had been in cahoots just now. But is it your contention you spotted a total stranger slapping leather behind another cuss you didn't know, and came unstuck that quickly with a shotgun you just happened to have handy?"

Cahill muttered, "Fuck you. Next time you can save your own life for all I care!"

Before Longarm could answer, they were joined by the shorter and thicker-set Sergeant Nolan of the Denver Police.

3

Nolan and Longarm went back a ways, so it was Cahill the blue-clad Nolan was covering with his own casually held six-gun as he moved in, asking in a voice of sweet reason, "And who might have been gunning whom on my beat this lovely morning, gentlemen?"

Longarm said, "Not me, Sarge. Meet Mr. Luke Cahill from Dallas, Texas. He says we're to call him the Caddo Kid and that this other one on the walk was fixing to shoot me in the back just now."

Nolan cocked a bushy brow at Cahill and growled, "We've heard about a bounty hunter called the Caddo Kid. Packs a private license signed by a Texas J.P. with no jurisdiction here in Colorado."

Cahill chided, "Bite your tongue. I'm no mere bounty hunter. I'm a recovery rider for a respectable, licensed bail bondsman in Big D and our jurisdiction extends throughout the nation!"

Longarm sighed and said, "Yes and no. When you agree to the usual bail-posting contract, you pay the ten-percent fee up front and sign away your usual rights under the U.S. Constitution. Your bondsman has to produce you or a death certificate in court on the day set for your trial, unless he wants to forfeit the bail he put up for you. So you have to agree in advance that you'll be there with bells on or he'll have your life, liberty, and anything else you got to dispose of as he and he alone sees fit. No arrest warrants. No extradition proceedings. Once you've skipped bail, you can offer your soul to the Devil because your ass will be grabbed by someone like Cahill here. He don't need a license or anything but a carbon of your bail contract to back his play as far as they want him to push it!"

Sergeant Nolan glanced down at the bloody corpse on the walk as he growled, "I know how it works. We have our own bail bondsmen over by the courthouse. So let me guess. This unfortunate who was about to gun a federal lawman for no reason at all jumped bail in Texas, and now he gets to ride home by rail, on ice, to satisfy his creditors?"

Longarm holstered his revolver with a weary sigh and said, "Sucker bet. But what do they care in Texas?" Smiling thinly at the so-called Caddo Kid, he said, "No shit, Cahill. What was he charged with down Texas way when he jumped bail?"

The burly Texan stubbornly insisted, "I wasn't after him. *He* was after *you*. Ask anybody you like and they'll all tell you I was sent up here after somebody entirely different!"

Sergeant Nolan decided that that was a good suggestion. Stepping toward the Overland Terminal, he opened the front door with his free hand and called out, "*Co Liam tha tu, agus a thig* out here on the damned double, Flynn!"

So little old Liam Flynn, the candy butcher who worked in their waiting room, came out with a shit-eating smile to ask if the darling sergeant had been talking about him.

Nolan snapped, "I was, and you should have come forward like a man, you Waterford Protestant! Where was you just now when this one on his feet put the other one on the ground and what could you be telling me about it all?"

The small gray candy butcher looked as guilty as if he'd done the deed himself as he confessed, "I niver seen either of them two before. Longarm here was known to one and all as he strode by without a word to anyone. Then the one on the walk stepped clear of all the ithers and went for his gun without one word either! I thought, Jasus, Mary, and Joseph, it's a killing I'm to witness! And I did! But it was this *ither* gentleman who was after shooting his friend in the back."

"Bull*shit* if he was any friend of mine!" wailed the Caddo Kid in a tone that made Longarm sort of glad that ten-gauge Greener's twin chambers still packed spent shells. The big bondsman waved the empty gun like a hickory stick as he insisted, "We were neither friends nor enemies! I've never seen him before! Find me one man in Denver willing to swear in court that he ever saw the two of us together, in sunshine or in shadow, and I'll suck his dick and stand drinks all around!"

Old Liam Flynn's continued survival on the blood-spattered

sidewalk had inspired others to gingerly come out of hiding as the last kitchen-match scent of spent gun smoke faded away and more copper badges arrived on the scene.

Longarm had been raised politely, and liked to think of himself as a fair-minded man. So after more than one other witness had backed the same story, Longarm grudgingly declared, "It pains me to say this. But there was this old-time English brain called William of Occam, and he had this imaginary razor he used to whittle away all the ifs, could-bes, and mayhaps until he was left with most-likely."

Nolan asked, "Who says anybody used a razor on anybody around here? This boy looks like he caught two charges of double-O buck in the back if you ask me!"

Longarm explained, "William of Occam's razor only slices away what seems unlikely. It seems unlikely these two boys could have been out to work together this morning, no matter how Texican they dressed for the occasion. It hardly seems likely a man known to track down bail-jumpers would gun a bail-jumper and act so modest about it. But let's see how thick or thin the *next* slice of the razor turns out."

Sergeant Nolan hunkered down by the dead Texas rider while Longarm innocently asked, "You say you were just standing here this morning with a loaded ten-gauge Greener, Mr. Cahill?"

Cahill replied easily, "Just call me Kid, or Caddo. I never said I was just standing here. I was fixing to board the next stage out for Julesburg. I don't know what that backshooter I shot in the back was doing here. Me and this old scattergun have to ride on up the line to see if a cook in Julesburg is the same French Canuck named Gaston who jumped bail down home after a mighty pointed argument with another boss."

Sergeant Nolan glanced up and declared, "You ain't going nowheres! Not before the Denver County Coroner decides whether we get to arrest you or not."

Cahill shrugged and handed his spent shotgun to one of the copper badges gathered around as he dryly asked, "Do you want to handcuff me now or can it wait till I'm indicted?"

6

Nolan got back to his feet, holding a wallet he'd found in the dead man's hip pocket. Nolan growled, "Don't be after sounding off and we might not have to split your skull, me Texas darling!"

Waving the open wallet in his hand, Nolan added, "I find it hard to believe that the one and original John Brown just tried to shoot you in the back, Longarm."

Longarm glanced down at the total stranger oozing blood and crud at his feet and decided, "A man with no more imagination that that might have fancied he could shoot a man in broad daylight, smack in the center of a fair-sized city, and still get away. I don't see how we'll ever get him to tell us why he was after me in particular. So much as it pains me to say it, I reckon I owe my continued existence to this other rough-hewn Texican, the Caddo Kid."

The Caddo Kid smiled bashfully and said, "Aw, I was only out to be neighborly, Longarm."

The just-as-tall but somewhat leaner federal lawman held out his right hand and smiled sincerely as he insisted, "No matter how you slice it, I have to allow you just now saved my bacon, and I have to say I owe you, Caddo."

The Caddo Kid shook. Longarm's hands were big because he was a big man. The Caddo Kid's right paw felt more like a smoked ham, and of course he tried to make Longarm wince by crunching down hard as he could.

When that didn't work, the Caddo Kid said, "I'm sure glad we have agreed at last that I saved your ass fair, with no ulterior motives. Because as a matter of fact, I might have one little favor to ask."

To which Longarm could only reply, "Name it."

Cahill said, "I told you gents I was bound for Julesburg to look up that cook we got a tip about. If this sideshow gives him time to get away, or it turns out he ain't the same Gaston as they sent me after, I'm going to need some guidance through your quarter here in Denver. They tell me you get along good with niggers."

Longarm dryly remarked, "That may be because I generally

refer to the folks who live in that part of town as colored. I thought you said this bail-jumping cook was a French Canadian."

The Caddo Kid explained they'd gotten the tip from a Pullman porter and paid for it by mail, in care of a house of ill repute in a part of town where a white Texas rider might not be well received.

Longarm told Nolan, "You all head over to the precinct house, and I'll join you there after I report in to my own office late as hell."

Then he turned to forge on, not looking back. But he hadn't gone far before Sergeant Nolan overtook him, saying, "Gilchrist and Ryan ought to be able to see a stiff to the morgue and a suspect to the precinct house. What have I been missing? On the face of it, the late John Brown knew you'd be headed for work this way on foot and—"

"How?" asked Longarm grimly.

Nolan was enough of a lawman to follow Longarm's drift. He gasped and replied, "Jesus, Mary, and Joseph, and it was only yesterday I heard about you and a new flame who lives on the south side of the City Hall! So most of your usual enemies should have been expecting you to follow a more southerly route from your furnished room, or a more northerly route from the brownstone of that widow up on Capitol Hill!"

Longarm kept walking as he quietly observed, "I noticed. It seems I have some new and *less* usual enemies laying for me now."

# Chapter 2

By the time Longarm had made his excuses at the Federal Building and made it to the precinct house, other witnesses had come forward to back the grim but simple story told by the so-called Caddo Kid.

An assistant D.A. examined Cahill's travel orders from that well-known Texas bail-bonding company, and decided they didn't want to make a fuss about a justifiable homicide.

The paper pusher who'd come over from the Denver Morgue asked for copies of everyone's depositions. He said they'd likely hold off on a coroner's inquest until they had a better notion of who the mysterious John Brown had really been. He said unless the dead man turned out to be somebody important, they'd likely agree with the D.A. and plant the poor bastard in Potter's Field without calling anybody in for direct or cross-examination.

So the Caddo Kid was off to Julesburg about that cook, and Longarm spent the rest of the day pulling bailiff duty in the courtrooms down at the far end of the Federal Building.

The firm but fair Judge Dickerson was presiding, and he was usually good for a hanging or at least some hard time. But business had been slow, and Longarm had to sit through a mess of motions for more time or lower bail. It gave him the chance to ask more than one private bail bondsman whether they'd ever heard of the Caddo Kid or his famous outfit down Texas way.

None of the Denver courthouse gang had heard of the Caddo Kid. But more than one allowed they'd dealt in the past with the Dallas firm called Triple 6 Associates. One old-timer recalled it as a finance or money-lending outfit that had branched into bail bonding down in Big D. Nobody had anything good or bad to say about them.

Longarm left for the day a tad later than he had to, and headed for his furnished digs on the unfashionable side of Cherry Creek in the tricky sunset light. Moving west into the sunset over the Front Range of the Rockies made it easy to suddenly stop in front of a shop window for a glance back to the east, where everybody's face was lit up like they were actors on the wicked stage. But he failed to spot any faces following him for more than a block or so. So he crossed the Larimer Street Bridge, strode on through the gathering darkness toward his known address until he was sure nobody was dogging him on the cinder-paved path, and suddenly cut between a Mexican *bodega* and some carriage houses to cross a vacant lot grown knee-high in tumbleweed, negotiate some alley doglegs, and recross Cherry Creek the hard way.

You didn't really need a bridge to get across the broad but shallow waterway the town had once been named after. When the water was low, you could hopscotch from one flat sandbar to another without getting your boots wet. So that was what Longarm did that evening, and in no time at all he'd threaded his way through other back alleyways to cut across the backyard of a hired bungalow on South Curtis Street and enter without knocking.

The petite but big-titted brunette shelling peas at her kitchen table looked up with a startled gasp as Longarm loomed there, framed by her back doorway. You could tell right off she had big tits because she liked to do her housework in the nude. That was another thing Longarm liked about her. She didn't blush or act flustered once she saw who it was. She dimpled up at him and asked, "What are you doing with your clothes on at this hour? Supper will be ready in an hour, and *I've* been ready since the City Hall clock struck six!''

That was another thing Longarm liked about her. Her name was Billie. She shut her own hat shop around five, and liked to get laid while her swell suppers were still simmering on her stove. So Longarm hung his hat and six-gun on a handy peg inside her door, bolted the door, and commenced to undress as he asked how come she was shelling peas so late in the day.

Billie said, ''They're for tomorrow. I thought I'd find something useful to do with my hands while I was waiting for you to handle the rest of me. Tonight's supper awaits your pleasure in the oven. But if you think we're going to eat before we fuck, you're out of your mind! What kept you all this time? I was starting to get worried!''

Longarm finished shucking his boots, stepped out of his tweed pants, and gently took the bowl of peas from her as she rose to face him and his enthusiastic erection. Then he had her on her back across the table, and she didn't ask any more questions as he treated her right, with his bare feet spread on the kitchen floor and her short strong legs wrapped around his naked waist.

Once he'd satisfied her that way, he naturally carried her into her nearby bedchamber to treat her even righter in a springy four-poster.

Billie kept her figure despite her healthy appetites for all of life's pleasures by indulging in them all as hard as she could. So she had Longarm out of breath and limp as a dishrag by the time she told him it was time to eat. To eat some *food,* she meant. She coyly added she'd save the French trimmings for dessert.

So Longarm got up and fetched his duds and six-gun from the kitchen while Billie loaded a tray with Spanish rice, Dutch apple pie, and Irish coffee. He hung the six-gun over the back of a bedside chair, and placed the double derringer from his vest pocket on the lamp table.

Billie waited until they were reclining face-to-face across

11

her bed with the grub between them before she asked if he was expecting a raid from the Denver Vice Squad. He told her the Denver Police didn't care whether such respectable residents had supper bare-ass or not, and tried to keep it as light-hearted when he went on to tell her about the shooting on his way to work that morning.

He'd been worried that a gal smart enough to run her own business might be as smart as him and Sergeant Nolan. Billie stared wide-eyed at him across the generously piled tray and asked, "How could anyone have been expecting you to cut through Tremont Place this morning, honey? Didn't you say you usually stayed over on the western side of Cherry Creek?"

Longarm washed down some of her spicy rice with her likkered-up coffee before he quietly answered, "Somebody has been gossiping about where I've been spending the last few nights. We'd better study about who'd know you and at least one desperate outlaw all that well."

Billie laughed in disbelief and said, "I sell hats to ladies of good taste and moderate means! Are you suggesting some desperado's doxie was watching the other day when you were kind enough to help us unload a delivery dray in that unseasonable rainstorm?"

Longarm considered how they'd met and discovered their mutual hankerings for late suppers and early loving. He hadn't been thinking dirty that Saturday afternoon when he'd seen a damsel in distress as he was heading for Capitol Hill in that gully-washer. He'd helped Billie and her shop assistant out of pure neighborliness, and that had likely been what surprised her when she'd invited him in afterwards to dry off over some hot cocoa and he'd simply allowed he'd take her up on it another time. Some gals just couldn't stand it when a man acted as if he wasn't about to come in his pants around them.

Thinking back, he failed to recall anyone at all on the rain-swept walk up on Broadway. But that wasn't to say that somebody couldn't have been tailing him at a distance, and anybody who had been, would have tailed him on up to Sherman Street and back on down the slope after a certain widow woman had slammed her damned door in his fool face.

Billie asked what he was grinning to himself about. So Longarm said, "The way things work out on rainy afternoons."

She smiled and sipped more Irish coffee before she coyly asked, "You mean the way you showed up at closing time, still soaking wet, and I brought you home with me, seeing my assistant had put out the shop stove and left for the day?"

Longarm answered, "Yep. I know you don't believe this. But I was as surprised to find myself suddenly hankering for that cocoa as you say you were."

She smiled like Miss Mona Lisa and murmured, "I wasn't really too surprised. I sort of thought you might change your mind, you gruffy hard-to-get man."

He had to laugh. But it would have been dumb to point out that another gal had been the one who'd changed his mind, or rather, his plans for that rainy afternoon. He still didn't know why his widow pal up on Capitol Hill had been so mean to him. He'd forgiven her as soon as he'd felt his old organ-grinder entering another fine port in that storm.

But that had been then, and this was now. So he cautiously said to *this* gal, "I never asked, and so you never told, whether I might or might not have taken you away from some other gent when I carried you home for that hot cocoa, Miss Billie."

She flushed all over and demanded, "Are you suggesting some old flame of mine hired that mysterious John Brown to do you in for having done me dog-style, you brute?"

Longarm grinned impishly and pointed out, "A jealous swain don't need exact positions spelled out on the blackboard of his mind, Miss Billie. I've seen men gunned on a dance floor just for asking another man's fancy for a Virginia reel. But you'd naturally tell me if there was some stuffy old husband I had to worry about, wouldn't you?"

She sobbed, "I told you that first night I'd been married to an older man of some experience and a weak heart. I *had* to when you implied I might have learned about blowing the French horn in some house of ill repute."

When he didn't answer, she insisted, "It's true, I tell you. I'd be lying if I said there haven't been just a few other men along the way. A warm-natured woman has needs, and dear old Clem had taught me to indulge them to the fullest. But I swear you're the only man I've made love to since I moved to Denver six weeks ago."

She absently rubbed herself between her crossed bare thighs as she added, "I was just about ready to go crazy with delivery boys when I caught up with you just in time. You know I'm a natural woman. Just as you're a natural man. But you're the only man I've ever fucked in the State of Colorado, and are you prepared to make the same claim?"

Longarm soberly replied, "Sure I am. You have my word I ain't never fucked one man in Colorado, or back in West-by-God-Virginia, come to study on it."

She didn't get it. Or perhaps she chose not to. She asked, "Why does your sleeping with me have to have anything to do with anybody anxious to see you dead, darling? My next-door neighbors may be sort of jealous. But one's a retired schoolmarm and the other's being kept by a married hardware salesman. Have you considered somebody might have been worried about that other Texas rider, the Caddo Kid?"

Longarm nodded and said, "Sure I have. That was about the first thing I went into with Luke Cahill. But as he pointed out, the one describing himself as a John Brown was aiming that Schofield at *my* back. Not nobody's back from Texas. Cahill cheerfully admits he's up here looking to capture a Texican bail-jumper. Any Texas friends of the fugitive French Canadian would have been as anxious to kill the Caddo Kid as *this* child. Gaston Dumas is the full name of the bail-jumping cook, and we don't have any federal paper on the surly brute. I asked when I got to my own office this morning."

Billie drained her cup and motioned for him to do the same as she tried, "What if they were afraid you'd help this Caddo Kid Cahill find that other Texan? Didn't you say *you* were afraid you'd be obliged to search the colored quarter with him

14

if he failed to catch up with his man over in Julesburg?''

Longarm drained his cup and put it back on the tray as he replied in an annoyed tone, ''I ain't looking forward to escorting a man who calls folk niggers to a couple of addresses I know. But nobody could have been out to backshoot me before I could help Cahill do anything at all here in Denver.''

Billie slid the tray off the bed and snuggled her naked charms closer to his renewed interest in such matters as she purred, ''Why not? How could you help the Caddo Kid give them a hard time if you were dead, dear?''

He asked, ''Why kill me to stop me from helping a rider I'd never met? It would have been as easy, and way safer, to gun a stranger from Texas instead of a Denver-based lawman smack in the middle of Denver. But speaking of giving any man a hard time . . .''

She snuggled even closer and took the matter in hand as she purred, ''I was so worried I'd served you too much Irish coffee, but heavens, is all this for little old me?''

He assured her it was as she rolled on her back, laughing, with her pretty little thighs flung wide in welcome. The cream and sugar she'd mixed in with that strong coffee and hundred-proof whiskey had restored his strength, while the supper break had allowed a man to get his second wind. So a fine time was had by all as he mounted her hot twisty torso and let himself go with her bare toes running through his dark wavy hair. She'd allowed that her next-door neighbors might be a tad jealous, and it was easy to see how any old gals who weren't getting as much might well be. For Billie moaned and groaned like a bitch wolf in heat as she invited the whole pack to have its wicked way with her.

He gently suggested, ''Don't *tell* 'em what we're doing. Let 'em just guess *some* of the details, honey lamb.''

But she kept yelling at the top of her lungs, ''Oh, yes! I love it when you hit bottom with every stroke, you astounding stallion!''

He muttered, ''Aw, now you're just showing off! You know I only hit bottom now and again when you really hug my ass with them astounding legs, you sassy little thing.''

She wailed, ''Come in me again! I love it when you come in me over and over, all through the night!''

He growled, ''I ain't likely to come once if you carry on that way, girl! If I wanted your neighbors keeping score on my coming and going, I'd invite 'em to come over and join us in one of them Roman rutting romps!''

So she promised to be good, and she was. He could hardly remember getting anything that good in recent memory. But once he'd come in her and come back to his senses, he sat up to light a three-for-nickel cheroot to share with her and inquire calmly, cuddling her back down on the pillows, how she'd known so much about the personal lives of those older gals to either side.

Billie answered simply, ''They told me. We girls talk about such matters just as much as you men do, you know.''

He'd known, ever since that neighbor gal back in West-by-God-Virginia had told half the congregation what he'd done to her in the church loft while home on leave from the war. He sighed and said, ''There you go. Most any gal in this part of town could have told most anybody in other parts of town I'd be headed to work by way of Tremont Place this morning.''

Billie didn't answer. She'd handed back the smoke and slither-kissed her roguish way down him to puff on something she'd described the last time as his West-by-God-Virginia perfecto.

# Chapter 3

Longarm didn't get too much sleep that night. But he rose with the chickens to get clear of Billie's back door before the sun came up. He followed Cherry Creek on down to Larimer Street, and made some show of breaking fast at a chili stand in the open-all-night arcade. He still had time for the haircut he'd been putting off before he showed up at the office way earlier than usual.

Marshal Vail and young Henry, the priss who played the typewriter out front, had naturally beat him to work. Longarm had never figured out why Henry did that. The thin pasty-faced squirt told Longarm the boss was in back, that a lady had left a message for him with the front doorman, and that the Texas Rangers had identified the late John Brown for them by way of a Western Union night letter.

Henry said Marshal Vail had the telegram from Texas in his inner sanctum. So Longarm settled for the envelope, which was colored lilac and smelled of familiar French perfume.

The handwriting was familiar too. Longarm still opened the fool thing on his way back to the marshal's office. Her message read:

*Darling,*

*Perhaps we've both been hasty and I hope you remember where I still live.*
*In anxious anticipation,*

The short message was signed with the outline of a heart. Society gals who anxiously awaited working stiffs seldom signed their names.

Longarm balled the lilac stationery up and held it as far as the private door marked UNITED STATES MARSHAL, FIRST DISTRICT COURT OF COLORADO. He went inside and asked the older, shorter, and stubbier gent smoking an evil cigar behind a cluttered desk in an otherwise neat oak-paneled office if he could use the wastebasket.

Billy Vail blinked uncertainly and said, "I reckon. What brings you here so early? You surely didn't run all this way from that hat shop gal to get rid of some secret love letter!"

Longarm laughed, and moved around to drop the crumpled message in the wastebasket on the far side of the desk as he replied, "Lucky guess. It seems I'm forgiven. Don't ask me why, or for what. Life's just too short to waste time trying to fathom the female mind. Henry says we got something from the Texas Rangers on the late John Brown?"

As Longarm moved back to the only seat on the visiting side of the desk, Billy Vail said, "His name wasn't John Brown. You say the young widow down Sherman from my house has forgiven you for spit-swapping with that hat shop gal, old son?"

Longarm sat down in the battered leather chair and fished out one of his own cheap smokes in self-defense as he wearily replied, "Nope. Never went near that new gal in town before that rich widow your own wife and her friends are worried about slammed her door in my face and told me to never darken it no more. I can't say why she treated me so mean. Like I said, life's too short, and we were talking about a man who tried to treat me even meaner yesterday morning."

Vail shrugged and said, "He was better known as Texas

18

Bob White when he rode with the Murphy–Dolan faction in the Lincoln County War. Never earned his keep as a hired killer down yonder. Signed on to herd cows for the Thompson brothers after Lew Wallace cleaned up New Mexico. Got fired for causing too much trouble on the trail. Didn't seem to savvy the finer points of herding cows. It's a long-established tradition that Texas trail hands bust up trail towns, not one another. Texas Bob tried to sign on as a railroad dick with the Pinkertons, but once again, a Pinkerton man is supposed to prevent trouble on the rails, not inspire it with rude remarks. The Rangers figure he might have hired on as someone's cheap private gun. He sure failed to earn his pay in Tremont Place the other morning.''

Longarm finished lighting his cheroot, and shook the match out as he soberly remarked, ''The one and original Caddo Kid opined the asshole seemed emotionally unstable. What's the story the Rangers tell on *that* Texican, by the way?''

The older former Ranger shrugged and said, ''Not much, for or agin. He really *has* been riding for that Triple 6 bail bonding outfit down in Dallas. The Rangers say they don't have anything serious on either Luke Cahill or the money-grubbers he works for.''

Longarm blew a thoughtful smoke ring and insisted, ''Not much adds up to a little. So what *do* they say about this Triple 6 outfit, Boss?''

Vail said, ''I said it wasn't serious. The state would have seized their escrowed surety and revoked their license if they'd done anything overtly crooked. The outfit started a few years back at bail bonding. It soon had a rep for recovering bail-jumpers a tad severely. Since they tracked down a few run-aways, the word on the street has been that you don't want the Triple 6 to go your bail unless you sincerely intend to show up for your trial. They've killed twice as many bail-jumpers as their next most ferocious rival down Dallas way.''

Vail took a meaningful drag on his own cigar, and then thoughtfully added, ''Luke Cahill, also known as the Caddo Kid, has killed more skippers for them than any of their other recovery riders. A baker's dozen or more. The Rangers only keep close tabs when you gun a man in Texas. There's many a small trail town in other parts where the contract a man signs with his bail bondsman is all the local coroner cares to look at before he issues you a death certificate to show the court clerk down Dallas way.''

Longarm blew another smoke ring and then, seeing Billy Vail had yet to provide an infernal ashtray for a smoking guest, he flicked his cheroot to treat the rug for carpet mites as he said, "Cahill would have asked for papers on Texas Bob, made out to the right name, if he'd been sent to gun *him* as a bail-jumper. So it's commencing to look like Texas Bob was really after me and had the bad luck to draw on my back with his back to a more sensible killer.''

Billy Vail nodded and said, "So we owe Cahill. Where do you reckon he'd be this morning, old son?''

Longarm said, "He lit out for Julesburg yesterday afternoon. I hope he found that French Canadian there. Cahill said he'd be asking us to help him find Gaston Dumas in our Denver colored quarter if he ain't where some Pullman porter said he'd be.''

He flicked more ash and added, "Before you ask, Cahill says Gaston Dumas is white. So don't ask me why he'd be hanging out closer to the colored railroaders who fingered him in the first place.''

Billy Vail had been hunting men on the run longer. So he nodded and said, "Cahill likely wants a word with that Pullman porter if they paid for a red herring. The Pinkertons use Pullman porters a lot too. A colored man fetching and carrying as he works you for a tip tends to fade into the varnish on a long cross-country trip, and a man looking over his shoulder for bloodhounds tends to forget a soft-spoken darky who saw where he got on and off the train.''

Longarm examined the smoldering end of his cheroot for sinister intent as he mused aloud, "I wish you hadn't made me consider that, Boss. I told Cahill true when I said I knew my way around our Denver colored quarter. I've noticed myself how often a colored waiter, maid, or whorehouse piano player remembers a white stranger in town with a furtive manner and a big bankroll. I don't want to lose any of my own friendly contacts in the quarter by introducing them to a man inclined to call folks niggers or pistol-whip informants for an honest mistake!''

Vail agreed they didn't owe Cahill that much, and suggested they lay down some rules before introducing him to any Colorado colored folks who might not admire the manners of that Texas cotton country along the Trinity. For despite its position not far from the Red River, the Fort Worth-Dallas Range lay a tad east of real Texas cow country, and a lot of Big D riders seemed to think out loud that a darky's place was way out in the cotton rows on foot. Some of the most notorious Texican badmen had gotten their start along the Trinity shooting colored men until they got up the nerve to shoot one another.

In the meanwhile, Vail wanted Longarm to keep up the good work down the hall in Judge Dickerson's courtroom. So the day proved to be tedious as hell, but as all things must, in time it got to where Judge Dickerson wearily called it a day around five and Longarm saw he might get an even earlier supper over at Billie's that evening.

But this was not to be. For Henry came to fetch him back to their own office before he could get away, and once there, he saw to his disgust that Luke Cahill, the Caddo Kid, was sitting and waiting for him in the outer office, without that Greener ten-gauge but armed on both sides with a brace of Colt '73's.

When he rose, they shook. Longarm had been raised politely, and the cuss *had* saved his bacon the day before. But when the Caddo Kid said he'd been screwed by an uppity coon and meant to put the black bastard back in his place, Longarm said, ''Not with my help, Caddo. As a sworn-in peace officer who owes you, I'd be willing to help you track down the bail-jumping Gaston Dumas. But as a man who spends more time here in Denver, I ain't about to aid and abet assault and battery on a Pullman porter who could have made an honest mistake!''

The burly recovery rider growled, "Nobody made no mistake. We were outbid by the bastard and his own nigger pals. The one I want to talk to about that has tipped us off to other bail-jumpers in the past. We have this understanding with some Big D darkies who've got kith and kin all over this land. When we put out the word about Gaston Dumas, the Denver darky who's a porter with the D&RG tipped us off he was up this way. We sent a money order ahead of me by wire, care of the D&RG, and the black rascal cashed it. But by the time I got here, he was boarding an eastbound run and left word Gaston Dumas was up in Julesburg, working as a cook."

"What did they tell you in Julesburg?" Longarm asked.

Cahill growled, "There was nothing to tell. Nobody there had ever heard of the bail-jumping Frog. Like I said, somebody's got to our finger man, and now I got to find him and set him back on the right track. But you have my word, I mean the boy no harm. No *personal* harm, at any rate. I'm sure I can get him to come to his senses and tell us where Dumas is really hiding out."

He saw the hesitation in Longarm's eyes and tried, "It would be dumb for me to lay rough hands on a Denver resident of color when I didn't have to. You'll see I know how to handle his kind, once you get me to the right colored whorehouse. His kind has a way of not offering the right directions through their quarter to strangers of any color."

Longarm asked what colored whorehouse they might be talking about. When Cahill told him, Longarm smiled dubiously and replied, "Madame Pickles's place ain't hard to find. I'll tell you whether I aim to carry you there after you've told me the whole story, Caddo."

Cahill tried to look innocent as Henry glanced their way from his desk across the way in sudden interest. Listening to Longarm trapping a bullshit artist could be fun.

The Caddo Kid tried smiling as innocently as a shit-eating dog. Longarm wasn't smiling back as he said, "I just spent a whole day listening to courtroom conversations. I wasn't paying as much mind the other day when you told me you'd come

22

all this way to carry a bail-jumper back to Texas. Our boss in the back verified your tale by wiring the court clerk in Dallas. But ain't you and your Triple 6 outfit stirring up a tempest in a teapot? Dallas says Gaston Dumas is really a cook with a nasty temper who really cut his boss over how you cook crawfish. After that, he got the charges reduced from assault with deadly to simple assault by agreeing to stand trial in Magistrate's Court without the jury the Constitution entitles him to.''

The Caddo Kid nodded, still smiling, and replied, ''That's the whole story in a nutshell.''

Longarm shook his head and insisted, ''No, it ain't. How much bail could Magistrate's Court impose with no prior convictions, a steady job, and facing no more than a year on the county roads? Five hundred, tops?''

Henry primly horned in. ''Two hundred. I sent and received all the wires, and we're not talking a full year at hard on a reduced charge.''

Longarm smiled thinly at the two-gun Caddo Kid and said, ''There you go. Your company would have made Dumas post at least twenty up front. So they're out no more than a hundred and eighty, written off as a bad debt. Correct me if I'm wrong, but ain't it throwing good money after bad to post rewards and send two-gun riders all over creation by rail after a petty offender?''

The Caddo Kid replied in a certain tone, ''You're wrong. How long would your average hooker feed herself and her pimp if the word got around that you could fuck her without paying in cash or blood? We ain't after Gaston Dumas and that cheating Pullman porter because they diddled us out of a little cash. We're after them lest word get around that you can diddle Triple 6 and hope to get away with it.''

He patted his right-hand gun-grip thoughtfully as he added, ''I mean to make that porter tell us where his newfound friend is really hiding out. Then I mean to carry Gaston Dumas back to Big D, dead or alive. He signed the contract. We meant to hold him to the contract he signed, lest others get the notion you can run out on us the same way. It's like the judge said about horse thieves. Horse thieves ain't hung for stealing horses. They're hung lest horses be stolen. See?''

Longarm shrugged and said, ''Not as clear as I'd like. You said that porter was boarding an eastbound run the other day when he told you Dumas was in Julesburg. So what makes you think we'd find him in any Denver whorehouse this evening?''

The Caddo Kid didn't hesitate. He said, ''Trains run both ways. My double-crossing darky ought to be back by now. If he ain't, I may be able to get something out of the other coons at Madame Pickles'. The bail-jumping Gaston Dumas likes dark meat and hangs around with more niggers than a carpetbagger running for office back in Reconstruction times. I figure some of his Texas niggers have put pressure on a Denver nigger we used to be able to trust. But I reckon I can make him see the light, and once I do, I'll just be headed back to Texas with that bail-jumping Frog, on his feet or certified dead for framing. Makes no mind to Triple 6, once a client's busted his word.''

Longarm glanced at the Regulator brand clock over Henry's desk and told the stranger in town, ''There's no action to speak of at Madame Pickles' in broad daylight, and gossip about white lawmen in the quarter could slow her business down considerably. So what say we move in after her regular customers have drifted in after sundown? Why don't we meet around eight o'clock in the Larimer Street Arcade near Cherry Creek? That'd give me time to have some . . . supper with a pal and explain about some night duty.''

They shook on it, and Cahill left first. Longarm smiled thinly down at Henry and asked, ''Have you ever had the feeling a friendly stranger on a train ain't sincere about that friendly card game in the club car?''

Henry sniffed and said, ''I don't play cards with strangers I meet on trains. Why go along with him if you suspect he's conning us?''

To which Longarm could only reply, ''That's easy. How else will I ever find out what he's really up to unless I go along with his con?''

# Chapter 4

They met at eight in the arcade, and they were crossing the Larimer Street Bridge over Cherry Creek when Longarm observed to the Caddo Kid, "No offense, but you are a stranger in town and I'd like you to keep it in mind that you won't meet many humble, barefoot, banjo-picking, former field hands where we're going. Colorado entered the Union with a clear conscience on the Peculiar Institution after siding with the Union during the war. The few colored folks up this way were free and fairly prosperous to begin with."

"I know how to handle niggers," growled the Caddo Kid.

Longarm answered simply, "George Armstrong Custer thought he knew how to handle Indians. My point is that they never grew much cotton to mention in these parts. So most of our local coloreds arrived as railroad folks or cowhands coming up the Goodnight Trail as free as their Anglo or Mexican *compañeros*. Ranchers in the western reaches of Texas had seen from early on how dumb it was to put a slave aboard a bronc with his own saddle gun, and there was no way an unarmed rider was about to hold your herd against Comanche and Mexican raiders."

The rider from more traditional parts of Texas sniffed and said he'd heard about them nigger-loving cattle barons west of the Brazos. Then he said soothingly, "Don't get your bowels in an uproar, Longarm. I told you I had no call to rough up any of your precious Denver darkies. When in Rome I can treat a nigger just like anyone else, as long as he stays in his place. The only bone I have to pick is with that lying porter, and I only mean to make him a better offer than the black friends of a white bail-jumper. How come there's no street lamps on this side of Cherry Creek if you Denver boys value the nigger vote so highly?''

Longarm smiled thinly and said, ''Nobody around City Hall worries much about *anybody* dwelling on this side of the creek, including *me*. The rents and property taxes are lower in this part of town because they never got around to paving or lighting up the streets this far from the Union Station.''

''You live in the colored quarter?'' marveled the Caddo Kid.

Longarm shook his head and said, ''Most of my immediate neighbors would be poor white or prosperous Arapaho, seasoned with Mexican. We're *headed* into more colored parts closer to the railroad yards. Like I said, a lot of colored menfolk work for the railroad or around the stockyards. You said you meant to make this porter on the D&RG a better offer than Gaston Dumas made him? I'm missing something here. Dumas skipped out on two hundred dollars in bail money to begin with. Why didn't he just send *you* the money if he didn't want to appear in Magistrate's Court on a minor charge?''

''We're not talking about *money*,'' said the Caddo Kid. ''Don't bother your pretty little head about it. It's a colored notion a heap of white men just don't understand.''

Longarm was tempted. But as he'd told Henry back at the office, he was unlikely to find out what was really going on unless he went along with it a tad farther. So he muttered, ''We turn west at that corner up ahead.'' And hardly noticed the tune he was humming under his breath.

Cahill had good ears. He said, ''I know that Sunday-Go-to-Meeting song,'' and proceeded to sing:

> Farther along, we'll know more about it.
> Farther along, we'll understand why.

Cheer up, my brothers. Walk in the sunshine.
We'll understand it all bye and bye.


Then he asked, "Why were you humming such a song at such a time and place, Longarm?"

To which the taller but leaner deputy could only reply, "Wasn't thinking about *why*. Thinking about *understanding* all this bullshit about some vast colored conspiracy hiding a white man to save him standing trial on a low-bail charge. It don't make a lick of sense to yours truly!"

The Caddo Kid said, "That's because you're thinking like a white *American*. Gaston Dumas is an infernal nigger-loving *Frog* who's found out how to get around black women and scare black men, see?"

Longarm didn't. So he led the way along dark and narrow unpaved streets to the surprisingly fashionable four-story frame house of ill repute near the coal yards of the Burlington Line. Some said Madame Pickles had paid to have her place moved on skids from more fashionable parts after a customer who was satisfied indeed had left it to her in his will. It sure looked out of place, looming in the moonlight above those hilly acres of coal out back.

One double standard of the late Victorians held that while a gal who strayed was a slut, it was only natural for men to rut like rabbits. Another unwritten but ironbound rule of the times was that while a black man asking for the services of a white whore was asking for a whole lot of trouble, North or South, a white man with the desire to change his luck was welcome at places such as Madame Pickles' as long as they knew he had the money and wasn't likely to make trouble. So the professor who manned the peephole drilled through the massive front door opened wide with a welcoming grin as soon as he saw it was Longarm who'd come calling with some other white.

Longarm wasn't known to them as a paying customer. They respected him more as a decent lawman who'd made more

27

than one arrest on the premises without busting up the furniture or calling any young ladies bad names. A towel gal ushered them into the downstairs parlor, a smoke-filled cavern furnished in red velveteen and mock mahogany, where they bellied up to the bar, as Longarm had suggested, to wait for the lady of color who ran the place to send for them or come out and join them. Madame Pickles liked to call the shots in her own sporting house.

It wasn't too obvious in the dim light, but close to a third of the other customers were white. Some dressed cow, and others were townsmen out for a night with "the boys." Which was the simple truth when you thought about it. When a bunch of the boys got a night out on the town, they tended to wind up at one whorehouse or another, and the white gals who whored for Madam Emma Gould or Madam Ruth Jacobs tended to look a lot like their wives at home had looked on their wedding nights. Besides, if a sassy young *colored* gal laughed at a middle-aged man's potbelly or limp dick, he could still feel he was her *social* superior, dad blast her uppity ways!

Madame Pickles chose to join them at the bar. She was wrapped in the same red velveteen she used for upholstery and drapes. It took a lot of red velveteen to wrap the middle-aged madam's elephantine form. But you could see she'd been pretty once, before she'd drunk all that booze and eaten all that grub. Her teeth were still pearly, and her high-yaller skin was still smooth over all that lard. So she might have meant it when she coyly asked Longarm if he and his pal were there on business or out to change their luck.

Longarm introduced the Caddo Kid, and explained what the recovery rider was after. She didn't seem to care. She said, "I knows the George you talking about, Cap'n. But he ain't here tonight. Somebody say he on a night run, fluffing up the pillows in his Pullman car."

Longarm knew the porter's real name might not be George. But *all* porters were George, in honor of Mr. George Pullman, their creator.

The Caddo Kid said he'd heard different, and said he'd just talk to some of her girls about that. Then he moved away from the bar before she could say yes or no.

Madame Pickles turned to Longarm with her face a calm mask as she said in a desperately casual voice, "You has to admire a man who knows what he wants. Are we going to have us a problem here tonight?"

Longarm truthfully replied, "I told him I wouldn't go along with one, Madame Pickles. Like I said, he's a guest from another jurisdiction and I owe him. He told me he only wants to talk to that Pullman porter about a bum steer. I reckon you'd have told us if you knew for a fact where that French Canadian bail-jumper might be, right?"

Madame Pickles looked away and said, "That white boy ain't Canadian French. He Creole French from Louisiana. What you drinking this evening, Cap'n?"

Longarm said, "Maryland rye if you got it. Are we talking about a Louisiana gentleman of color, Madame Pickles?"

The immense quadroon shrugged her plump bare shoulders and told him, "Creole be French spelling of Spanish Criollo, for white folks born on this side of the main ocean in colonial times. Ain't *supposed* to signify colored blood. But don't you ever call a Mississippi Delta Cajun a Creole if you don't feel like fighting. Cajuns is really pure French who got moved down from Canada one time by the king of England. Gaston Dumas looks white as you, but he ain't no Cajun. He likes dark meat, *whatever* he be. That George spotted him here in this parlor a week ago, sparking one of my ladies in French. I got three who really hails from Louisiana, and two more who just *say* they French and charge extra for French lessons up in the cribs. You want us to give you any French lessons, Cap'n? Like I've told you before, anything I can do for the law is on the house!"

The yellow gal tending bar in a thin chemise slid his Maryland rye and a tumbler of branch water across the zinc top of the bar as Longarm smiled fondly at his gracious hostess and said, "One of these evenings I'll take you up on that and likely shock us both. The Caddo Kid says that after your other customer wrote about Gaston Dumas being here in Denver, he seems to have had a sudden change of heart and sent the Kid on a wild-goose chase. What can you tell me about that?''

Madame Pickles shrugged again and said, ''That Creole boy pay the house rates and don't make no harsh demands on the Louisiana ladies he likes best. Maybe somebody tell that George he shouldn't have the law on such a friendly ofay.''

''Or maybe somebody told that porter they'd clean his plow unless he changed his story,'' Longarm decided. It had been a statement rather than a question, but Madame Pickles allowed that made sense, and added that she took little personal interest in the talk that might go on upstairs.

Then a stark naked and very black whore with eggplant tits made a liar out of Madame Pickles by coming down the stairs with her eyes as big and white as two boiled eggs, screaming, ''Grigri! That Texas ofay after Gaston lay a grigri on me and I too young to die!''

Madame Pickles whirled on Longarm to demand in an accusing tone, ''Whuffo you lie to me about that Texas grigri man passing for white?''

To which Longarm could only reply that he had no idea what she was talking about. He asked, ''What in tarnation is grigri? Is it anything like that voodoo you hear about down along the Gulf Coast?''

Madame Pickles snapped, ''Voodoo, hoodoo, mumbo jumbo, or grigri is all the same bullshit to *this* child! I was brung up by Holy Rollers! But that bad white boy you carried through my front door be really bad if he lay any of that bullshit on a *believer* like Violet here!''

She asked the naked, shivering Violet what the Texan had laid on her and what she'd told him. Violet whined, ''Goofer dust! He pour goofer dust in his palm and say he gwine blow it over me if I don't tell him who that Creole boy wiff. So I tells him he wiff Francine and then I come down here to tell you-all!''

They were still digesting that when another naked lady of

30

color came down the stairs yelling, "Cap'n Gaston gwine out the back wiff the devil on his heels!"

So Longarm charged past the foot of the stairs to tear down the hallway, through the kitchen, and out the back door just as a fusillade of pistol shots rang out not far away!

As Longarm had foreseen, the Caddo Kid had chased his quarry out the kitchen door and across the small back garden into the coal yards rising in the moonlight across a crooked alley. Longarm had his own gun out as he forged up the nearest slope for a better vantage point, calling out, "Where are you, if you're still on your own feet, Cahill?"

He heard the Caddo Kid call back, "Over this way, closer to the tracks. The stupid bastard wanted to make a fight of it and guess who won!"

Longarm followed his own gun muzzle across the rolling hills of Colorado coal to where the Caddo Kid stood tall in the moonlight with a smoking Colt '73 in each big fist. He stared down at a frailer figure sprawled head low, stocking feet high, and face up—that is, if he'd had much of his face left.

Longarm joined the truculent Texan to stare morosely down at the late Gaston Dumas, who'd died with his boots on a whorehouse floor after fleeing in just his pants and undershirt. Something gleamed in the moonlight, further down the slope of moonlit coal. The Caddo Kid said, "He pulled a gun on me. I think that must be it yonder."

Longarm moved down the slope, noting in passing that the dead man had been shot up a lot after going down. There was no way to put that many rounds of .45-28 in a man who was still on his feet.

The two-dollar whore pistol further down the slope appeared to be a Harrington & Richardson .32. Longarm left it where it lay for the Denver Police to study. Moving back up the slope, he called out to the Caddo Kid, "If it happened as you say, you were right about his lack of common sense. What was he facing back in Dallas if he'd gone back with you peaceably? An added charge of fleeing justice, worth mayhaps ninety more days at hard in addition to forfeiture of that two-hundred-dollar bail?''

The man who'd just filled the fugitive full of lead replied in an uncaring tone, ''I reckon. A man would have to be mighty stupid to jump bail on a minor charge to begin with. But you can see he did, and so I did what I had to, and I'm counting on you to back me up with the local powers that be, pard.''

Longarm dryly remarked, ''I figured you might be. I call things as I see 'em. So whilst we wait here for the arrival of the Denver Police, you'd best fill me in on this voodoo shit you just pulled back yonder in that colored house of ill repute.''

The Caddo Kid holstered one six-gun and began to reload the other as he said, ''I just do what my outfit orders me to do. I told you how that nigger-loving bail-jumper got to that Pullman porter with his own black magic. We got our own expert on the subject, helping my Triple 6 outfit whenever we run into such problems. She gave me some goofer dust and told me how to use it, did I want to scare the truth out of any Denver darkies, see?''

Longarm said, ''I'm commencing to. Whatever you used on shy Violet sure worked. What's in this goofer dust you blow at naked whores to make them tell you so much?''

The Caddo Kid said, ''How should I know? Do I look like a voodoo witch doctor? Most of the *niggers* don't know much about voodoo. You only run across it where West African slaves were owned by the French in days gone by. But former slaves in general seem to be scared out of their wits by voodoo notions. So who am I to argue?''

# Chapter 5

Denver County never saw fit to indict the Caddo Kid for killing a couple of vaguely sinister strangers in town with no visible means of support. So that seemed the end of it, as far as Longarm was at all concerned. But as long as he was stuck that week with courtroom duty, he borrowed some books on mythology and superstition from the Denver Public Library to read whenever things got really tedious in court. A man could only stay halfways alert when they had a prisoner before the bar, and it seemed lawyers liked to jaw on and on with nobody sworn in or even in the blamed room.

So by late that afternoon, Longarm had finished the one book and had had a good skim through the second when Judge Dickerson got down to the more serious business of sentencing a man who'd gotten to be a serious cattle baron by stealing other folks' cattle.

Longarm set his library books aside and stood with his back to the wall near the main doorway, watching the crowd instead of the bench, as the fair but firm Judge Dickerson sentenced the cow thief to twenty at hard in Jefferson Barracks.

The gray-haired defendant wailed, ''You can't give me that much time in prison, Your Honor! I'm already sixty-four years old! I'll never live long enough to do twenty years at hard labor!''

Judge Dickerson beamed down at the elderly cow thief and said in a soothing tone, "You just serve as much of the time as you can then. Case closed, and I want Deputy Long to join me in my chambers now."

So as they led the weeping and wailing cow thief away, Longarm made his way back to the chambers, hoping they weren't going to have a tedious discussion about Miss Bubbles from the stenographers' pool down the hall. Longarm had warned Miss Bubbles the judge's chambers were a piss-poor place to suddenly offer a man a blow job.

But the steel-gray jurist seemed friendly enough as he shucked his black poplin robe to take a seat behind his desk and shove a box of Cuban claros across the desk to Longarm, explaining that he wanted to jaw about that double killing Longarm had been mixed up in a few days ago.

Longarm took a seat and helped himself to a claro as he sheepishly replied, "I never fired a shot, and I ain't sure you could describe the separate incidents as a double killing, Your Honor."

Judge Dickerson said, "Sure I can. I get to describe things any way I want to because I'm so distinguished. I read both the newspaper and coroner's accounts, Deputy Long. On the face of it, a recovery rider here in Denver to catch a bail-jumper just happened to notice another gunslick throwing down on a federal lawman, namely you, and then just a little over twenty-four hours later he catches up with his original quarry and has to shoot him in front of namely *you*. Doesn't that strike you as stretching coincidence, Deputy Long?"

Longarm got the mild Cuban cigar going and shook out the match as he replied easily, "Me and Marshal Vail figured he was lying through his teeth, Your Honor. But we've wired high and we've wired low to establish any motive for the Caddo Kid to backshoot Texas Bob. Or for Texas Bob to backshoot me, for that matter. We weren't able to find any. Somebody might have paid Texas Bob to lay for a lawman in Denver, but the Caddo Kid didn't get a plugged nickel for plugging Texas Bob."

34

"As far as you know," Judge Dickerson pointed out after a thoughtful drag on his own cigar.

Longarm blew a luxurious smoke ring and replied, "Me and Marshal Vail have turned that notion every which way, Your Honor. If we reach way out yonder for any profit to the Caddo Kid in shooting a madman or a paid assassin, why would he want to *hide* it? Others who were there agree Texas Bob was drawing on my back and had it coming. The Caddo Kid made no bones about it being him as shot Texas Bob. He made sure Reporter Crawford of the *Denver Post* spelled his name right. Had he wanted to shoot Texas Bob on the sly, he could have done it whilst they were both in Texas. Had he had any other reason for shooting Texas Bob so publicly, he would have been free as a bird to offer it."

Judge Dickerson regarded the ash of his claro thoughtfully as he said, "Set that shooting on the back of the stove and return with me now to that killing out back of that whorehouse."

Longarm nodded and said, "Oh, that amounted to an execution, Your Honor. He told us up front he'd been sent to bring Gaston Dumas back to Dallas dead or alive. I suspect, and Marshal Vail agrees, that he asked me to tag along that night so's he'd have a white lawman as witness to his purity of heart. I told him I considered it mighty tacky to toss a two-dollar whore pistol down the slope after he caught up with that bail-jumper and saved his outfit a first-class ticket by returning Dumas as a death certificate. But Denver County didn't care, and the Caddo Kid owned up to shooting that bail-jumper for profit. There wasn't no reward money posted on Gaston Dumas. Cahill says they pay him by the month whether he brings in one or a dozen."

Longarm removed the cigar from his teeth and quietly added, "I never asked, but I gathered they'd fire him if he failed to bring back anybody they sent him to bring back."

Judge Dickerson grimaced and said, "That Triple 6 outfit sure has had a heap of bail-jumping. They lose money on each such incident no matter how they finally turn the culprit over to local courts. So how can they stay in business, and have you ever heard that 666 is the number of the Beast, or His Satanic Majesty?''

Longarm patted the library books in his lap and replied, ''I have, Your Honor. So I've been reading up on such subjects, and to begin with, our Devil ain't *their* Devil.''

''Whose Devil *is* numbered 666 then?'' asked the older white man.

Longarm said, ''Satan, meaning Enemy in Hebrew, Your Honor. Devil is Latin for a lesser god. His name is Legion, from Lucifer to Old Nick or Mister Scratch, but he's still the white man's Devil and it ain't true that voodoo is devil worship as we'd understand the notion.''

''You've been studying that voodoo religion of the Delta darkies?'' asked Judge Dickerson, marveling.

Longarm said, ''Just since another white man used such notions to scare the liver and lights out of some Delta darkies who'd been hiding a white Creole who'd been slick enough to evoke Mamba Dyumbo, the tribal spirit as protects homes and villages, or punishes womenfolk who break tribal laws, such as the laws of hospitality. Some white folks who think they know more than they really do about some colored folks call Mamba Dyumbo *Mumbo Jumbo* and get the notion all wrong.''

He took another drag on the claro and went on to explain. ''Voodoo is our spelling of the French Creole *voudou,* which is closer to the West African *vodun,* meaning a spirit. Any spirit, good or bad. Madame Pickles told me Cahill laid a grigri on her Lousiana voodoo followers to counter old Gaston's obeah. This one book ain't too clear on just how grigri and obeah are different. But from the way they were talking, *they* must feel, at least, that an actual grigri charm, such as a bag of goofer dust, has more power than the *notion* of obeah, which sort of translates as sorcery. I've noticed it's tough to translate Indian words such as *wakan* into English too. *Wakan* makes as much sense in English if you call it medicine, power, or mystery. But I've heard a medicine *bundle* has more power than a medicine *chant.* So I reckon old Gaston used an oral spell, and Cahill topped him with that goofer dust you could see and smell.''

Judge Dickerson insisted, ''Goofer dust issued by the number of the beast, and I've heard a thing or two about this voodoo-hoodoo devil worship too! I don't think it's fair to blame African witch doctors for all those wicked rites wherever slaves were owned and influenced by French Papists. You never heard plantation hands on the Tidewater tobacco or Carolina rice plantations singing anything more sinister than 'Swing Low, Sweet Chariot!' Bond servants tend to ape the manners of their masters, and it was the Roman Catholics who held inquisitions into devil worship, right?''

Longarm dryly replied, ''Yep. It was *witchcraft* the good Protestants of Salem village charged them elderly women with, after a West Indian slave gal told a bunch of bored white brats about obeah. No offense, Your Honor, but when it comes to damn fool superstition, there's enough to go around, whether the fools are white or black, praying in the woods or in any other breed of church!''

Judge Dickerson said soothingly, ''Don't get your bowels in an uproar. I never said I believed in horsefeathers either. My point is that the folks running this 666 bail-bonding operation seem to!''

Longarm shrugged and said, ''I ain't sure, Your Honor. The Caddo Kid admitted using goofer dust, but called it nigger superstition. Dallas squats half in and half out of the cotton country where a heap of old-timers, black and white, set store by voodoo, obeah, and such. Gaston Dumas used obeah he'd learned somewhere in trying to get away from the gents who'd posted his bail money. So knowing at least a little about such notions must come in handy down yonder where so many folks believe in it.''

Judge Dickerson sighed and said, ''I wish I knew why. Apparently sane white women pay ragged-ass Gypsy women to read their fortunes as well. Do you recall that passage in Mr. Hugo's book about Notre Dame where Miss Esmeralda, the

Gypsy gal, asks how come her folks have to camp out by the side of the road, living on handouts, if they have real magic powers?"

Longarm nodded soberly and declared, "Made sense to *me*. But some folks seem to feel a bare-ass Indian medicine man who can't read or write has to know more about curing white folks than white doctors. I asked a white lady from New Orleans how they'd ever *held* slaves with the powers to cast spells on anybody they didn't admire. She told me I just didn't understand. She was right. I'll be switched with snakes if I can see why a man with the powers of life and death at his own command would be out there chopping cotton under a hot sun. But when you ask why some folks believe in such bullshit, you're putting the cart before the horse, Your Honor. Some folks of all ranks, and poor folks in particular, *want* to think there's some shortcut to fame and fortune. They know they ain't likely to get anywhere any other way."

Judge Dickerson made a wry face and said, "That Triple 6 outfit must be banking heavily on the number of the beast then. I don't see how *else* they expect to get anywhere. I've been in touch with other jurists to the north and west of Texas since I read your report about that shooting the other night. Triple 6 has an astonishing record when it comes to going bail for Texas badmen. At ten-percent interest, no bonding company can afford to forfeit more than ten times out of a hundred to break even. But the Caddo Kid and some other recovery riders cut from the same cloth have had to bring back close to a fifth of their clients who'd jumped bail!"

"Dead or alive?" asked Longarm quietly.

The judge said, "Fifty-fifty, with Cahill and another colorful recovery rider called Lash Legrange accounting for most of the death certificates. Their outfit's operating at a loss in either case. You don't get the bail money back whether a later date is set for a bail-jumper's trial or the case is closed for other causes, such as sudden death."

The judge took a drag on his cigar and added, "The one called Lash Legrange gunned a bail-jumper hiding out with a

Black Seminole squaw in the Indian Territory. So Judge Parker over to Fort Smith sent a couple of his own federal deputies down Dallas way to go over the books with some court clerks. They didn't find out too much. Triple 6 is the brand of a cattle spread and the trademark of a bonding and money-lending corporation owned by the same old Texas family. Their handle would be Wedford, and they say they lost a granddad over at the Alamo in '36. Other partners in the Triple 6 financial operation are all white Protestant stock with deep Texas roots.''

Longarm was about to say that seemed sort of suspicious on the face of it when the aptly named Miss Bubbles from the stenographers' pool swept in with a yellow Western Union form and an innocent expression in her big blue eyes.

The bubbly blonde in shantung smiled at Longarm and handed the wire to Judge Dickerson as Longarm idly wondered whether His Honor had ever had her on that leather chesterfield against one oak-paneled wall. Judge Dickerson didn't stare after her as the warm-natured little thing left the room, with her globular rump swinging like a saloon door on payday.

The judge read the wire, grinning like a mean little kid. Then he told Longarm, ''Your old pal the Caddo Kid saw fit to detour through Dodge on his way back to Dallas. Seems another bail-jumper had been seen more than once in the Long Branch. Only they met early this very morn in the alley behind the Alhambra, and this time the both of them lost.''

He set the wire from Kansas aside as he continued. ''As of high noon today, they were both clinging to life in adjoining hospital beds after gutshooting one another at close range. Luke Cahill or the Caddo Kid just passed away, but as I'd been hoping he might, the bail-jumper who shot it out with him is still alive and expected to last at least a a day or so.''

Longarm nodded and asked, ''You want me to run over to Dodge and see what he has to say before he follows the Caddo Kid down yonder where they both should have known they were headed?''

Judge Dickerson looked disgusted and replied, "Why, no, I expected him to leave us a sworn deposition. His name's Taylor. Charles Edward Taylor, and the charge they'd bailed him out on was a less lethal shootout in a Dallas dance hall. The Sheriff's Department over to Dodge has the paperwork Cahill was carrying on Taylor. It must not be true that a dying man has nothing to hide. Taylor keeps saying he never heard he was wanted in Texas, never jumped bail anywhere, and thought Cahill was out to rob him when they met in that alley and the Caddo Kid slapped leather first."

Longarm decided, "Nobody is that fast. They both knew one another on sight and knew it was time to go for their guns. I'll catch a night train and see what else I can get out of him. But what if he dies on us without coming clean?"

Judge Dickerson shrugged and said, "You catch the next train back and we wait for another break."

"Sounds tedious," Longarm remarked, going on to calmly suggest a course of action that left the older man staring goggle-eyed.

Judge Dickerson gasped, "You can't be serious! Even if Marshal Vail was willing to let you risk it, I could never ask him to send a lone deputy into such a dangerous situation!"

Longarm pointed out, "No offense, Your Honor, but we'll never savvy the situation at all unless we take advantage of the one break we've been offered by Lady Luck up to now."

# Chapter 6

Dodge City, Kansas, was the seat of Ford County, leading to some overlap of municipal and county law. The state legislature over in Topeka had just voted Kansas dry. The sheriff, town law, and saloon keepers on both sides of the Dodge City Dead Line agreed they'd never heard such nonsense in their lives. Abilene had gone dry a spell back, and Abilene hadn't seen a herd in town since. So the powers that prevailed in Dodge put nothing in writing, and tended to be sort of evasive when strangers in town stuck their noses into local matters.

This suited Longarm to a tee as he played the matter of the Caddo Kid out by ear. He wasn't a total stranger to Dodge. So a pal in the Ford County Sheriff's Department got him into their small county hospital, a sort of glorified clinic of whitewashed frame construction upwind of stockyards.

Longarm's train from Denver had pulled in well after dark. So the coroner had long since released the body of the Caddo Kid to a local undertaker who specialized in shipping thoroughly embalmed cadavers in sealed lead-lined coffins. But Ford County had hung on to the Caddo Kid's six-guns and recovery papers, which named the old boy who'd shot him as a Charles Edward Taylor who'd jumped a hundred-dollar bond on a penny-ante disorderly shooting charge. Longarm had already seen the brace of Colt '73's Cahill had been toting. So he paid more mind to the papers the recovery rider had been toting. Then he and his pard from the Sheriff's Department, Deputy Will Connors, went upstairs to see what the soon-to-be-late Chuck Taylor might have to say for his fool self.

It was easy to see he wasn't long for this world. The prim-lipped nurse who led them to the dimly lit death chamber on the top floor said they weren't to get her patient excited. Chuck Taylor looked as if he didn't have enough life left in him to get excited if they all stripped stark naked and sang "Marching Through Georgia." He was wrapped in tight bandages from his hip bones to his floating ribs, and smiling wanly at somebody else in the room they couldn't see, as Longarm told him he'd never seen a man gutshot over such a small amount of bail money before.

The dying man—they said he was a contract trail herder when he wasn't dying—shook his head weakly and replied, "I never jumped no bail, high or low. I was telling the crazy coot that when he drew on me ahint the Alhambra. He had the wrong hombre, the murderous son of a bitch!"

Longarm quietly replied, "I figured you had to have some advance notion he might draw on you. Let's not worry about who went for his guns first. I just now went over the bond contract you signed with that Triple 6 outfit down Dallas away, Mr. Taylor. I'll allow two riders could be named Charles Edward Taylor. I'll allow they could both be known along the same trails as professional drovers, and I'll go along with you both being tall, rangy, and sandy-haired, if you'd like to tell me how come you both sign your names the same way. The signature on the contract Cahill was carrying matches the signature you left in the registration book at the Manhattan House Hotel, no offense. That recovery rider can't hardly tell us now, but I've been known to go over hotel registers in a trail town after I'd heard some fugitive I was trailing might be there."

Chuck Taylor shook his head stubbornly and asked—reasonably as soon as you studied on it, "Why would I be signing my right name in any damn books if I'd even suspected I might be wanted by any law? I cheerfully own up to getting

42

a room in the Manhattan House under my true name. I never signed bail-bond papers under *any* damned name! They must have *forged* my name down in Dallas, see?"

Longarm didn't. He said, "Mr. Taylor, the late Caddo Kid had a written agreement, signed with your John Hancock, before he got to Dodge and commenced to ask around town for you. Are you asking us to buy some complicated forgery scheme when it works so simple another way?"

Deputy Connors chimed in. "He means you'd be the one and original bail-jumping boy from Dallas County. We've already checked by wire with the court clerk who's named on the papers Cahill had on you. So don't try and wriggle out of that disturbance of the peace in the Red Mill Dance Hall near the Cotton Exchange. You made a Mex dance indeed, and scared everyone half to death that evening, cowboy."

Taylor weakly insisted, "I never did. If I had occasion to draw on any greaser, I'd have aimed at his belly. Same as I aimed at that lying son of a bitch ahint the Alhambra more recent. I never shot up no Red Mill Dance Hall in Dallas. I didn't know there *was* a Red Mill Dance Hall in Dallas! The only such place I've heard tell of is the one in Paris, France, where them frisky cancan gals don't seem to need nobody shooting into the floor around *their* high buttons."

Longarm had to smile at the frisky scene Taylor evoked as he said, "If we buy some other Charles Edward Taylor raising Ned in that other Red Mill, then signing himself out of night court with a mighty convincing duplicate of your usual signature, how do you account for a grown man with a lick of sense choosing to shoot it out rather than pleading 'Not Guilty' in an open court to a minor charge? Seems to me, a man who'd never been to any Red Mill in the first place ought to get off easy when no witnesses showed up to prove the contrary."

The dying man sighed. "I was afraid they'd lined up some *false* witnesses against me."

Deputy Connors demanded, "To what end, old son? We're talking a noisy but non-lethal disturbance of the peace charge, with no more than ninety days in the county jail if the judge had a real hard-on for you! Don't it stand to reason that if there'd been some vast and mysterious conspiracy to frame you, they'd have framed you as a bank robber or at least a horse thief? Why would anyone want to accuse you of little more than malicious mischief, stand you a lousy hundred bucks in bail money, and—''

"They wanted an excuse to kill me!'' Taylor cut in, adding bitterly, "They done it too. The nurses keep telling me they're waiting on the doc to give me something for the pain. But we all know there ain't no way to make it stop hurting now! I never done nothing to nobody, and here I lay with a belly full of bullets and Mr. Death grinning at me from them shadows over by the door. Somebody paid that Caddo Kid to pick a fight with this child and clean his plow with .45-28 slugs. I knew he was out to kill me the minute he called me on owing his boss a hundred dollars. I didn't know him, didn't know his boss, and never borrowed no hundred dollars from no-body!''

Deputy Connors quietly observed, "Says you do, right on that bond contract we found on Cahill right after you shot him.''

Taylor moaned, "What do you think he was doing to *me* at the time, massaging my scalp? Nobody paid me to gun him. They paid *him* to gun *me*. But why are we arguing about that? According to that old grinning cuss over yonder, I ain't never going to have to prove doodly-shit in any court of law.'' He rose on one elbow to smile insanely at the gathering darkness as he called out, "I'm ready to ride anywheres if we can leave this pain ahint, Mr. Death!''

The nurse came in to shoo the two lawmen out. Connors might have argued, but Longarm murmured, "Let's go. We're talking circular with a dead man who ain't about to change his tale of woe.''

Connors agreed a nightcap over at the Manhattan House made sense. As they went dowstairs and headed over to the bright lights of Dodge, Longarm said, "I'd be obliged if nothing about out call upstairs this evening made any papers, pard."

Deputy Connors said, "Done. I was up there alone just now, as I recall. Not that I got anything *new* out of him. He's been telling it the same way since they drug him in, dying, this morning. That recovery rider made the usual courtesy call on the town law when he got into Dodge about this time last night. So *his* tale stayed the same, both before and after he caught up with his man and the two of them had it out at point-blank range over a hundred dollars!"

Longarm said, "Cahill told me the idea was to keep others from feeling they could cheat his bail-bonding outfit. Even when you threw in the savings of this detour to Dodge, his travel expenses must have topped the combined bail money Taylor and the late Gaston Dumas owed. Hanging drifters for stealing stock has a wondrous a way of getting others to think you mean business."

Deputy Connors said, "Read about that shooting in the Denver coal yards in the *Kansas City Star*. You were there, weren't you?"

Longarm shrugged and kept walking as he replied, "Sort of. As in this most recent gunplay, we're stuck with the version the Caddo Kid, or in this case his target, testifies to. If things happened over in Denver the way the Caddo Kid said, the late Gaston Dumas wasn't half as good with a gun. Does Taylor back there have a rep as a gun?"

Connors thought and decided, "Not a hired gun or even a mean gun, now that you ask. But they allow he's killed his man. More than once. Shot a man in Abilene a few years back over cards, and another down in San Antone, I think, over a woman at a dance. His point's well taken that he'd rather aim at man's guts on a dance floor than down at his boots. You reckon it's possible they got him mixed up with some less lethal dancing master?"

Longarm answered, "Don't know. I'll ask aroud the Red Mill once I get there."

"You're going on down to Big D?" marveled Deputy Connors.

Longarm shook his head and said, "Not tonight. Got to wait for the poor boy to die. Then I hope you can sneak me his death certificate and at least a notarized facsimile of those papers the Caddo Kid was carrying on him."

As they reached the steps of the sprawling Manhattan House, Longarm soberly added, "I'd be obliged if you could have 'em delivered here to Mr. Nero Culpepper in Room 206. I don't want to be seen around the county courthouse come morning, seeing I left for Denver on that midnight westbound tonight."

Deputy Connors chuckled and said, "The long arm of the law moves in mysterious ways. Are we talking about Crossdraw Culpepper? Bounty hunter who went too far and wound up in the Colorado State Prison?"

Longarm led his fellow lawman through the street entrance to the hotel taproom as he replied, "My friends just call me Cross, because of the way I pack my pistols. After that, we both hail from the same hill country on the far side of the Big Muddy, and whilst we ain't at all related and don't really look to be twins, we'd describe much the same as tall, dark, and handsome."

Connors laughed and said, "Always said you had more balls than a brass monkey. But what if the real Crossdraw Culpepper escapes, or a rich uncle gets him out whilst you're in Dallas pretending to be him?"

They bellied up to the bar as Longarm quietly explained, "I don't expect either to happen. The real Crossdraw Culpepper just died of consumption in the prison ward. Some others pals who ride for the State of Colorado say they don't have to make a big public display of it. Culpepper was an orphan and a one-woman man whose one woman killed herself when he was sent away for life. Other pals on the *Post* and the *Rocky Mountain News* have agreed to hold off on any obituaries for the time being in exchange for personal interviews once I get back, *if* I get back."

The barkeep drifted their way as Deputy Connors declared in a dry, sarcastic way, "It's good to know you're back in business, Cross. Badmen from here to the border will be hiding under their beds as soon as word gets around that they pardoned you for shooting that bitty kid in line with a wanted man's back. But I have to say I'm just as glad you ain't after nobody here in *Dodge,* you murderous cuss."

Longarm told the barkeep they'd both have bourbon and branch water. He'd already asked for rye there, and the shit they'd served had been a piss-poor imitation of real Maryland rye.

Their Kentucky bourbon was tolerable, and the water tasted as hard most anywhere on the High Plains. As the barkeep drifted off, Connors said in a more sober tone, "It ain't gonna work. We've heard our own tales about that bail-bonding outfit Cahill was riding for, and the so-called Caddo Kid did seem to be cut from the same cloth as the murderous Crossdraw Culpepper. But outfits in the market for a hired assassin ain't likely to hire any off the street, are they?"

Longarm downed half his bourbon, chased it with half the branch water, which was really well water in those parts, and told the less experienced lawman to his left, "Gents in the market for a hired gun have seldom thought it through. Neither faction down in Lincoln County, New Mexico, should have thrown together private armies of mean and crazy cowboys. Tunstall and McSween on the one side wound up dead, and neither Dolan, the late Major Murphy, nor the late Sheriff Brady got a thing to show for all that gunplay. We've heard over in Denver that most of the serious killings in the name of that Triple 6 outfit were the work of the late Caddo Kid and another gun waddy called Legrange, Lash Legrange. So unless that wasn't so, they've lost fifty percent of their guns, and I don't aim to just walk in and apply for a job. Playing a trout on a line, flirting with a lady on a train, or getting in with a gang calls for much the same delicate moves."

"You're fixing to get yourself delicately killed," Deputy Connors warned, draining the last of his own nightcap and adding that he had a hot meal and a fairly warm wife waiting for him across town.

So they shook and parted friendly. Longarm watched Connors leave, and casually glanced around for the barkeep. He spotted the beefy and sort of shifty-eyed cuss talking to a less-well-lit female over in a corner booth. Whoever she was, she had on widow's weeds and a veiled hat. Longarm didn't care. He hadn't wanted a second nightcap that hard in any case. So he left a dime tip by the empty glassware and strode into the next-door lobby, where he casually waved to the key clerk and headed on to the stairwell. As a seasoned traveler, Longarm kept his hotel keys on him instead of occasioning extra work for everyone every time he went in or out. Most key clerks were just as glad.

He went on upstairs, and casually made certain the match stem he'd wedged in a lower door hinge was still there. He unlocked the door, and went in to find the roping saddle he'd borrowed from the Diamond K was still draped across the brass foot of the bedstead with his Winchester saddle gun getting along fine, lashed to fresh surroundings.

Longarm shucked his hat and coat, unbuckled his gun rig, and sat on the bedcovers to shuck his boots. He had one boot off and one boot on when there came a gentle rapping on his chamber door. What flapped in when he opened up, six-gun in hand, looked more like a woman in black than a raven. She gasped, "Shut the door! I don't want anyone to know I've come to you, you dreadful man!"

Longarm shut and bolted the door to the hall as she removed her hat and veil to reveal a vision of blond loveliness. She was about the same size and almost as curvy as Miss Bubbles back in Denver. But she looked twice as smart and seemed far more ladylike, until she told him flat out, "I want you to kill a man for me. I'll give you all the money I have and if I have to throw my body in with it, so be it. I'll give you eight hundred dollars and all the fucking and sucking I can manage, if only you'll shoot Simon Fuller for me!"

48

# Chapter 7

Her name was Bernice Durler and she was the recent widow of Link Durler, shot down like a dog over in the stockyards by Simon Fuller, a trail boss and notoriously mean drunk from Fort Worth. Longarm learned all this in the time it took him to sit back down and haul that other boot on.

The Junoesque young widow woman remained standing as she tossed her veiled hat on the dresser and got to work on the buttons of her black bodice, cursing Texicans in general and Simon Fuller in particular under her breath.

Longarm calmly told her, ''I wish you'd leave your duds on, ma'am. I've read Ned Buntline's Wild West magazines too. But there just ain't no incorporated township where you can shoot a man down like a dog and walk away scot-free. How come you haven't taken your complaint to the town marshal or county sheriff, both to be found within walking distance.''

She went on unbuttoning as she sobbed, ''I did! As soon as I got word my poor Link had been murdered over the price of beef! They said all the witnesses there agreed Link drew first, after Simon Fuller called him a cheap Damnyankee bastard. All those witnesses were Texas cowhands, and why shouldn't my Link have reached for his gun after he'd been called a bastard in public?''

Longarm sighed and replied, "For openers, it seems he was a tad slow for a gent acting so insulted by a man with a rep. When did all this unfortunate gunplay take place, and will you *please* put that bare tit back in your bodice, Miss Bernice?"

She exposed the other tit, along with both bare shoulders, as she told him Simon Fuller had made her a widow more than six weeks earlier. He was inclined to believe her. But before he got to comforting any warm-natured widow woman who hadn't been warmed of late, he felt obliged to warn her, "I don't shoot men for love nor money unless they have some wanted papers out on 'em, Miss Bernice. You get me an arrest warrant from any district attorney, coroner, or even constable in Kansas, and I'll be proud to haul old Simon in, dead or alive. But I'm a bounty hunter, not a paid assassin, and who *told* you I was a bounty hunter, by the way, that nosy barkeep down in the taproom?"

She went on undressing as she demurely replied, "He knew of my distress. The gunfighter I'd been meaning to hire, another Texican trail herder called Chuck Taylor, was killed less than twenty-four hours ago by some friends of Simon Fuller!"

Ignoring her naked charms with considerable effort, as she sat down beside him stripped to the waist, Longarm said, "No offense, but that might not be exactly the way it happened, Miss Bernice. The man who killed Taylor and vice versa was working for a bail-bonding outfit. It seems Chuck Taylor was wanted in Texas for another feud entirely. Why would friends of this Simon Fuller want to stop a gunslick you hadn't hired yet?"

She said, "I'd sent out word I was in the market for any man who'd take up my just cause. More than one I talked to suggested Taylor as a known enemy of Simon Fuller. It's true they both had reputations as Texas badmen. And they'd clashed over water and rights-of-way on the trails to the south. So I thought—"

"Poor Charles Edward Taylor will never know what he missed out on," Longarm said. "He ain't expected to live through the night, and that barkeep who told you I'd just got out of prison after doing hard time for another shooting wasn't listening as tight as he should have before he went blabbing around town about this child!''

She leaned toward him, her nipples leading the way, as she sobbed, ''Please help me, Crossdraw! Somebody has to avenge my murdered man! And I don't know how long Simon Fuller will be in Dodge City this time! We thought he'd gotten away for this year when he rode south a few days after killing my man. Then we heard he was back with a herd of black Cherokee longhorns from the Indian Territory, and—''

''You're talking to the wrong cuss, as hot and bothered as you have me!'' Longarm declared as he rose to his feet and unbolted the door. ''I mean to open this door to a public hallway on the count of ten, Miss Bernice. You do as you've a mind to. But if I was you, I'd have my tits put away before the count of eight or nine!''

He started counting with his hand on the knob as she flustered to her feet and made herself presentable with a speed and grace that spoke of practice. But she stayed put, looking more dignified, begging him loudly, as he opened the door, to kill Simon Fuller for her.

It wouldn't have been polite to yell back that a lady was *loco en la cabeza*. So Longarm gently but firmly ushered her out as he repeated his suggestion that she call the local law against anyone she was at feud with. She couldn't seem to grasp that a bounty hunter who'd just been let off early from a life sentence might hesitate to slap leather on a total stranger for another total stranger. She protested that she'd been trying to know him harder, in the Biblical sense. But he finally got rid of her, and made sure the barrel bolt on his hired door was a solid one before he finished undressing and climbed into bed with the intent of a good night's sleep after a long hard day.

It would have been easier to fall asleep if he hadn't seen that beautiful blond widow woman's tempting tits. But a man who'd lay wild false claims to being a hero just to lay a gal was more of a shit than one who paid cash and tried to convince himself it was true love.

51

He made himself speculate on what sort of a home spread he meant to have in the distant future, once he got old enough to retire and start a family with that ideal gal who'd be a master chef in the kitchen, a perfect lady greeting friends in the parlor, and a total slut greeting him in the bedroom after they'd gone home.

Building castles in air had a way of digging a tired head deeper into the pillow. So the next thing Longarm knew, a steam locomotive was ringing its bell right outside his window, and when he sat up to swear, it was daylight outside. So he got up, pissed in the chamber pot, and took a whore bath at the corner washstand before he got dressed. He figured a man who'd just got out of a state prison would dress less fussy than the Reform Administration of President Hayes and his prim First Lady, Miss Lemonade Lucy, would expect from a deputy marshal on duty. So he broke out some clean but faded jeans and an old blue bib-front army shirt from his saddlebags, and strapped his regular cross-draw gunbelt over the more casual outfit.

He wore his usual coffee-brown Stetson and stovepipe cavalry boots because you could tell at a glance whether a stranger was wearing a new hat and boots, and he didn't want anyone speculating on his general appearance for no good reason. He put the pocket watch and double derringer he usually wore on either end of a chain across his vest in a hip pocket, once he'd unclipped the handcuffs he usually packed on the back of his gunbelt and put them away in a saddlebag. Then he went downstairs to see if they were serving breakfast yet.

They were. He'd just dug into his flapjacks with sausages under a lot of thick but mild sorghum syrup when two other early risers came in, talking about Charles Edward Taylor and that other dead man from Texas.

The Caddo Kid's corpse was waiting at the freight depot in that lead-lined coffin. They were holding a morning service for Taylor because, even though he'd been another pestiferous Texican, he'd had a gal in Dodge who'd cared more for him than anyone down Texas way seemed to.

Longarm knew his secret pals in the Sheriff's Department would see that he got the papers he wanted on Taylor, now that Taylor was dead, if he'd just sit tight and wait for a discreet delivery. There was no safe way for a well-known Colorado lawman, pretending to be a less well-known bounty hunter, to sashay over to the courthouse and ask them to hurry it up. So he topped off his flapjacks and sausage with apple pie and extra black coffee, enjoyed an after-breakfast smoke, and drifted out front to see what in thunder might be holding up the damned delivery.

Most of Dodge City was strung along a mighty broad main street divided by railroad tracks smack down the middle. The famous McCoy stockyards, railroading facilities, and heavier shopwork, such as the smithies, saddle shops, wagon wrights, and so on, lay south of the line along with cheaper boarding-houses, gin mills, and quick-service cribs. It wasn't true that the "Dead Line" formed by the tracks called for anybody getting killed if they crossed it. Dodge City existed to serve the cattle trade anything it wanted at any price it was willing to pay, anywhere in town. It was simply understood that visitors to Dodge, as well as the whores and gamblers who lay in wait for them, would not get away with unseemly behavior north of the tracks, where the prices as well as the customs were fancier. Pissing in the street south of the Dead Line was one thing. Pissing in the street north of the Dead Line could land an old boy in jail with cuts and bruises.

As he stood on the veranda of the Manhattan House, smoking a fresh cheroot, Longarm heard a commotion down the way and craned for a look-see. It was a funeral procession, headed for the Prairie Grove Cemetery.

Longarm didn't know whether that was the late Charles Edward Taylor in the rubber-tired hearse or some other unfortunate. In any case, no Dodge City funeral procession would be heading for "Boot Hill." For that was yet another dirty little secret of the dime-magazine writers.

There wasn't any Boot Hill in Dodge City. An ad hoc Potter's Field on a slight rise to the northwest of the much smaller

Buffalo City might have been dubbed Boot Hill by the buffalo hunters and whiskey drummers who'd camped for an informal time five miles west of Fort Dodge. But the coming of the Santa Fe rails in '72 had mushroomed the former wide spot on the Santa Fe Trail to a settlement of twelve hundred more or less permanent residents, incorporated as Dodge City, "Queen of Cow Towns" or "Babylon on the Plains," with two theaters and better than a score of respectable saloons, along with countless houses of ill repute, fly-by-night card houses, and opium dens that came and went as the respectable ladies north of the Dead Line demanded, whenever they heard one was there. None of this activity called for a Potter's Field inside the city limits of a mushrooming town. So the more formal and refined Prairie Grove Cemetery was laid out as a public burial ground, and those few unfortunates actually planted in the original Boot Hill were moved as far downwind as everyone else to free up the prime real estate in town for first a schoolhouse, and more recently the new City Hall.

But to read Ned Buntline, you'd never think the Dodge City Hall sat atop any temporary Potter's Field, and tourists were always asking to see those comical grave markers described by reporters such as Ned Buntline or Frank Leslie—as if anyone with a lick of sense and a desire to go on living would bother to carve a mocking epitaph for a dangerous man with friends, who might be able to read, still up and about. Reporter Crawford of the *Post* had told Longarm that some photographers had started selling postcards with such droll inscriptions as "He called Bill Smith a liar," or "Drew too slow in an unfriendly game of cards," the photographs taken, they said, at some Boot Hill in some Western town. It only took a few minutes to burn such nonsense into a plank with a soldering iron, and you could drive that plank into the 'dobe soil of any handy vacant lot.

A gal in black was following the hearse, riding sidesaddle on a black pony. She looked to be part Mexican or maybe colored. Once breeds lightened up to almost white, it was tough to determine what one or more grandparents might have been. She sure was pretty, though.

Some other kith or kin were following her respectfully. Longarm spotted Deputy Will Connors back a ways on a paint pony, and decided that had to be Chuck Taylor in the hearse. They'd said Taylor had had a local true love, and it was funny, once you thought about it, how the Caddo Kid had seemed to track down bail-jumping white boys with colored pals, or colored folks he thought were pals.

Boot heels and a set of spurs that really jingled were coming along the planks behind Longarm. So he stepped back against the hotel wall to clear the right-of-way as he turned with a casual smile.

The burly figure in bat-wing chaps and a high-crowned dove-gray sombrero didn't walk on past. He stopped a yard and a half away to demand in an oddly high-pitched twang, "Might I have the honor of addressing the one and original Crossdraw Culpepper, the terror of the North Range?"

Longarm went on smiling, but it wasn't easy as he answered in as casual a tone as he could manage, "My friends call me Cross and I ain't looking to terrorize nobody, Mr. . . ."

"Fuller. Simon Fuller, and it's come to my attention that you have been looking for me," replied the drover, who'd obviously started to drink early. He snickered and added, "I thought I'd come looking for you and save you the trouble, you son of a bitch!"

Longarm went on smiling as he quietly replied, "I'm going to let that pass this time, Mr. Fuller, because I fear we've both been the victims of a big fibber. You have my word as a man that I have not told a living soul I am after you. I have no call to be after you. I don't know you and you've never done me wrong, assuming I overlook that rude remark about my possible ancestry."

"You don't feel so brave now that we're face-to-face, eh?" asked Simon Fuller owlishly.

Longarm didn't answer. There were times nothing one said

to a woman or a drunk was going to do you a lick of good, and this seemed to be one of those times.

Simon Fuller swayed on his high heels as he taunted Longarm. "Let's see how good you are in a man-to-man showdown. I ain't no kid you can gun in the back, Mr. Crossdraw Culpepper I've heard so much about! I am here this sunny morning to call your bluff! It's been said around this town that you've come all the way from Colorado to have it out with me, and I'm saying here and now I don't think you have the sand in your craw for a fair fight with any man!"

Longarm said, "Have it your way then. Feel free to tell all your friends and relations that you ran me out of town. Because I'll be leaving town this very morning and—"

Simon Fuller slapped leather.

He was wearing his Remington-Rider .38-30 low in a tied-down *buscadero* rig before he gave himself the edge by deciding when to open the festivities. So, drunk as he was, he beat Longarm to the draw.

Then, drunk as he was, he missed his first shot at point-blank range, and never got the chance to fire another. For Longarm, better known that morning in Dodge as Crossdraw Culpepper, blew the mean drunk from Fort Worth off the veranda and down in the horse shit and dust of Main Street with one round of .44-40 delivered where he'd aimed it, smack between the eyes.

You had to make sure a man died quickly when he was aiming his own smoking six-gun your way at that range.

# Chapter 8

So there, it seemed, went a carefully laid plan Billy Vail had said he'd never get away with. He had the faked papers to back his tall but logical story, and the man he'd just had to shoot had sure been convinced he was the one and original Crossdraw Culpepper. But any lawman questioned by the law was supposed to tell the truth, and now town and county law was approaching from all sides, together with a considerable motley crowd.

Knowing anyone in the gathering crowd could be a pal of the dead man sprawled in the dust at his feet, Longarm kept his .44-40 out as he got ready to produce his federal badge.

Then Deputy Connors, bless him, called out, "I saw the fool draw and fire first, Crossdraw. But what was it all about?"

Longarm lowered his six-gun's muzzle politely, but kept it handy as he called back, "Can't say. Don't know. Jasper said his handle was Simon Fuller and allowed we were at feud. I'd just told him I didn't see why, when, as you say, he drew on me and I done what I had to."

A town lawman sidled up to the sheriff's deputy and muttered under his breath. Longarm could hear the quick-witted Connors replying, "His name's Culpepper. Bounty hunter. Just got out of prison after another shootout in other parts, the poor cuss. You know how it gets once a man has a rep and every mean drunk he meets wants to see how good he really draws!"

Coming closer, Connors said, "Show Deputy Marshal Tweed those same prison release papers you showed me, Crossdraw."

Longarm produced the fake papers his other pals at the Colorado State Prison had typed up for him. He didn't have much choice unless he wanted to make a liar out of Deputy Connors and explain a mighty tangled web indeed with half of Dodge City listening in.

The funeral procession had moved on, although some of the party had stayed for what promised to be a more interesting morning. As the town law looked over the fake papers and travel orders home to the Cumberland hills east of the Mississippi, Deputy Connors was growling, "You'd best come with me and see if we can't clear this up with the county before noon, Culpepper. You heard the sheriff tell you last night that we didn't want to see the sun set on you more than once in Ford County, you troublesome cuss."

"I didn't start it," Longarm complained, as if he was Crossdraw in truth. One of the townsmen in the crowd volunteered, "That's true. I seen the whole thing from across the way. That cowboy in the gutter drew and fired before this other gent got his own gun out!"

A youth dressed like a cow hand opined, "Old Simon was a hard man to talk to when he'd been at the corn squeezings. You mind that cattle buyer Simon started up with six weeks or so ago?"

A townsman objected, "That was different. Link Durler drawed on Fuller that time."

The young cowhand insisted, "Same difference. Simon called the man a cheap Damnyankee bastard, and worse than that, a liar. So I say both fights were started by the same mean drunk."

The town law handed the release forms back to Longarm and soberly said, "What's done is done and yonder lies one Texan who won't start any more gunfights in *this* town. If the

58

county wants the case, I ain't about to argue. The paperwork can be so tedious when there's neither bounty money nor tickets to a hanging in prospect!''

Connors said, "Come on, Culpepper. You and me better talk this over with the sheriff, if not the district attorney.''

Longarm reloaded his revolver and put it away as he followed Connors away from the scene. The town law bawled after them, "Hold on! Who's stuck with this dead body if you don't want us to handle the case?"

Connors called back casually that he'd send the county morgue crew to tidy up. Nobody tried to stop them as they strode on out of earshot and left most of the crowd behind. A dead body oozing blood while it gathered flies was more interesting to study on than a pair of grown men walking soberly.

Connors led the way as far as the Comique Theatre, where he swung them into the alleyway to the stage entrance, saying, "Come on. I know the manager and we can hang around backstage until things calm down outside. Meanwhile we can send a boy to gather the possibles you left at the Manhattan House. You *were* fixing on catching that noon eastbound, weren't you?"

Longarm dryly replied, "I'd better, if I mean to transfer to the Gulf Coast line. How am I supposed to thank you right without getting all mushy, pard?"

Connors said, "Aw, don't go getting mushy on me. I ain't interested in boys that way. I want to get us off the streets and out of sight before my watch commander can ask me what I think I'm doing. I ain't aiming to get mushy with you in the dark, you pretty little thing.''

Longarm laughed and said, "Go ahead and play hard to get for all I care. Didn't you tell that deputy marshal out front of the Manhattan House that you'd send for the county meat wagon?"

Connors replied simply, "I did. I have. Sent a kid in the crowd to fetch the coroner's boys on the double. By the time they get the body over to the morgue and someone gets around to asking who filed the report to begin with, nobody but us will know where to find us officially. I'll naturally have to file a report in triplicate, once I get asked for one.''

Longarm nodded in sudden understanding and said, "I have to handle my own boss like that sometimes. Old Billy Vail would just as soon not know we're bending the rules until after we've bent them without serious breakage.''

Connors led the way to a stage door barely ajar to the alley breeze as he said, "Won't nothing be broke if the transient Crossdraw Culpepper has left town before anyone ordered me directly to hold him for that pesky inquest. The coroner's jury can manage well enough with all the witnesses to Simon Fuller's nasty temper that I can produce easy.''

The elderly doorman inside shot them a quizzical look through the slot he was guarding. Connors said, "You know me, Pops. We're here to investigate a complaint about pink tights with strategic holes in 'em.''

The old-timer chuckled and let them in as he allowed he'd been wondering where he'd lost his fool pecker.

All theaters seemed to smell the same backstage. It was dark, and somewhere a piano was playing while high heels thundered on a hollow-sounding stage. Will Connors led Longarm sideways to the noise along a passageway leading to a spiral staircase as he said, "Old Ed knows I'm a married man and thinks I'm screwing around with some dancing gal in the troupe. So he won't tell anyone he's seen me today unless they produce a search warrant and point a gun at him.''

Longarm asked how come as they went up to a hidey-hole where some folding chairs occupied a niche behind fake organ pipes. The Ford County lawman said, "I sided with the management at the inquest after the ushers bounced an unruly patron a mite too hard one evening. He was wearing a gun as well as in love with a lead singer. So we got them off on self-defense.''

They sat down and lit up as Longarm saw he had a sort of view of the stage below. The thundering herd of dancing gals in gym bloomers seemed to be having a tough time with the piano man, or vice versa. He'd play about eight bars as they all tried to stay in step. Then he'd stop, cuss in a high and bitchy voice, and yell, "Once more!" so they could all bounce and jiggle to those same eight bars of what might have been a cakewalk. It was hard to tell what a dance troupe had in mind when they kept stopping and starting over. A bunch of dancing gals were a lot like cavalry on parade. The results were pretty and looked easy, but they took a lot of practice.

Will Connors leaned back expansively and said, "That pleasantly plump strawberry blonde, second from the right flank, is the one old Ed thinks I'm screwing. I heard she puts out too, and there are times a man wishes he could be single again for just one night. But a deal is a deal, and I've never strayed since me and old Beth married up two years ago come Midsummer's Eve. What's the story about you and that Widow Durler, Crossdraw?"

Longarm sighed and said, "I see the late Simon Fuller wasn't the only gent in town who knew she'd been to see me last night. That two-faced barkeep must have told everyone who had a beer there after he'd sent her up to recruit the famous hired gun. But like I was trying to tell Fuller when he drew on me, I told the lady I wasn't fixing to kill a man I had no quarrel with, for love nor money."

"Which did she offer?" asked Will Connors.

Longarm sighed and said, "Both. Said she'd give me eight hundred dollars and her fair white body if I'd avenge the death of her man. I never saw the money, but she showed me enough of her fair white body for me to assume she meant it. How am I supposed to get my saddle and other possibles from that hotel if I'm to catch that train in time?"

Connors said, "Let me worry about that. Reporters and likely friends of Simon Fuller may be watching for you to come back to your hotel for your things. I don't want you out in broad day until just before your eastbound starts loading. I'll get you there on time, and one of the ushers downstairs will have your gear waiting for you on board. Leave such petty details to a man who knows the ropes around Dodge. What else might you know about that tempting young widow woman's quest for vengeance? Fuller killed Durler six or eight weeks ago, and from what you tell me of her persuasive powers, I'd have thought she'd have had Fuller killed before you ever got here under any name!''

Longarm smiled thinly and said, ''She told me she had that bail-jumping Chuck Taylor lined up for the job. We never got around to any exact terms of that deal. She said Fuller had been out of town for a spell and then, just as she'd recruited Taylor to do him in, the Caddo Kid and Chuck Taylor killed one another behind the Alhambra. She had the notion Caddo was a pal of Fuller's. That has to be pure bull, of course?''

Will Connors nodded, then frowned thoughtfully and said, ''I follow your drift. You said that Triple 6 rider was in Dodge on detour after completing a job for his outfit in Denver. *He* said he was after Chuck Taylor for bail-jumping. He even had the papers to prove it. But eight hundred dollars and a piece of Bernice Duller would tempt *this* child if he wasn't married up and not a hired gun!''

Longarm thought and decided, ''Those court papers Cahill had on young Taylor point the other way, and who was that true love riding a black pony behind his hearse this morning?''

The lawman, who knew the whole county better, didn't hesitate as he replied, ''That's Muskeegee Rose. Owns a tea parlor and reads tea leaves for more than she charges for tea with scones. She blew in from the south six months or so ago, and they say she does right well with her tea and fortune-telling parlor. I can't say just when she and Charles Edward Taylor got to be so friendly. They were sort of discreet. He was known around town as a trail herder who came and went as his fortunes dictated. Muskeegee Rose must not have read his fortune worth spit, albeit he must have been on the prod the other morning when he bumped into the Caddo Kid in tricky light and they both drew and fired about the same time!''

Longarm took a thoughtful drag on his cheroot and said, ''He told us Cahill had no call to throw down on him. But you're right about him moving mighty fast for a young cowboy with nothing on his mind but a visit with . . . Who? Why would a man so friendly with a mighty pretty fortune-teller be out on the dark streets of Dodge at that hour?''

Connors tried, ''Mayhaps seeking other fortune. Bernice Durler told you she was trying to get him to gun Simon Fuller for her, and after a man's been having chocolate for a while, he might fancy a few dips of vanilla.''

Longarm nodded soberly and said, ''I noticed the female mourner on that black pony was sort of dusky. When they call her Muskeegee Rose, are they being mayhaps a tad delicate about her true ancestry?''

The lawman, who knew the lady better, said, ''Hell, I don't even know if that's her real name. Whatever she is, she's mostly white with a little Indian blood, or what they call a dip of the tar brush down in Texas. They had colored freemen as well as slaves under the Peculiar Institution west of the Brazos. But lest somebody suspect granddad might have been a slave, the Texicans of color prefer to be thought part Indian or even Mex. Up close, Muskeegee Rose could pass for a Gypsy gal, and sometimes she lets her patrons suspect she might have secret Gypsy powers. I'll be switched if I can say whether she's part Gypsy, part Mex, part Muskeegee, or just *passing,* as they put it when they don't want to own up to being, say, an octoroon.''

Longarm grimaced and asked, ''Who could blame 'em? You'd never call a Dutchman with one great-grandmother from Ireland an Irishman, or a Spaniard with a great-grandfather from Sweden a Swede. But some folks can sure get picky as soon as all the great-greats ain't pure white.''

He took another thoughtful drag before he asked, ''Have you heard tell of any voodoo spells or mayhaps bags of grigri goofer dust being served with tea by this mysterious Muskeegee Rose?''

Will Connors laughed incredulously and demanded, ''Served to white ladies in *Kansas*? You ain't supposed to sell 'em hundred-proof medications for their female complaints, if the truth be known. Muskeegee Rose just reads the bitty black tea leaves left in the cup after a silly old patron swills it. Voodoo is that superstitious nigger shit from the Gulf Coast, right?''

Longarm said, "Close enough. These books I read say it started in Haiti among French-speaking African slaves. Seems they enslaved some priests and priestesses of spirits called *voduns* whilst they were at it. Such notions mixed with French Papist rituals, some of them held backwards as if to spite the white saints, have blended into voodoo, as it's better known along our own Gulf Coast, where the folks used to carry on in French.''

Will Connors pointed out, "Some still do, and you're mixing me up. What in thunder might this voodoo shit have to do with gunfights here in Kansas, for Gawd's sake?''

Longarm shrugged and said, "Can't say. Don't know. But the Caddo Kid used voodoo shit in Colorado to find one bail-jumper, and the bail-jumper he caught up with here in Dodge was mighty friendly with a lady of at least possible color who for certain peddles magic.''

Connors objected, "Come on. Fortune-telling ain't voodoo, is it?''

Longarm replied, "Neither one qualifies as *logic*. Folks who believe in one brand of magic tend to believe in others. Muskeegee Rose might be selling magic under some other name, but under any name it smells much like any other mumbo jumbo, hoodoo, voodoo, or whatever the hell keeps cropping up in this fool case!''

# Chapter 9

Had there been easy rail connections through the Indian Territory between Texas and the more built-up rail grid to the north, nobody at all would still be bothering with long trail drives. But thanks to the War Between the States, the longer Reconstruction, and a depression back in the '70's, Texas had been behind the door when the railroads were being handed out. They were just now starting to get some fairly long shortline railroads across the vast expanses of the Lone Star State, and so Longarm had to hairpin south and change to stagecoaches for a few legs of his weary journey before he finally got off in Dallas with his borrowed stock saddle and possibles, needing a bath, a shave, and a haircut.

He checked into the Travis Hotel, and treated himself to a long, hot tub bath. But although he changed to clean underwear and a fresh shirt, he decided to stay a mite unkempt for now. One of the few advantages the fussy dress code of the Hayes Administration offered a federal lawman was the simple fact that these days everyone expected them to turn up neat.

Locking his baggage in with a match stem wedged under the bottom hinge of the door, Longarm had a late breakfast of chili con carne under fried eggs, with a slab of chocolate cake and black coffee to hold things in place, before he headed for the Ranger station between the City Hall and the municipal corral.

As in the case of the late-blooming railroads, the choice of sides the Lone Star State had made during the war had stunted the growth of the Texas Rangers considerably.

The Texas Rangers had been organized as a force of fifteen full-time Indian fighters back in the 1820's. By 1835 there were about 150 such riders, and they got their title of "Texas Rangers" during the revolution against Mexico. By this time they were ready to take on Comanches, Mexicans, outlaws, or anybody else they got asked to. So they naturally took on the Union Army as part of Hood's Texas Brigade, and that was one Ranger mission that didn't go so well.

The Texas Rangers were disarmed and disbanded by the occupation army of the Reconstruction, to be replaced by the hated "Texas State Police," federally funded and, like the army of occupation, partly if not largely made up of ex-slaves with many a grudge to settle. So the predictable results had been the Ku Klux Klan and the beginnings of many a Texas gunfighter's rep.

But tempers in higher places slowly cooled, and in '74 the federal governor of Texas allowed Major John B. Jones to reactivate a frontier battalion to handle Quill Indians and desperados, while the Special Force under Captain McNelly patrolled the border with its former firm grip on the reins.

But some of the features of the Reconstruction had lingered on into the current Administration of Rutherford Hayes, who'd been a decorated Union general the Radical Republicans couldn't describe as a copperhead when he'd ended Reconstruction entirely.

Once they were back in total control, some Texicans and many a Ranger made no bones about "damnyankeeniggerlover" being one word, indivisible by hyphens or common sense. To some unreconstructed Texas Rangers, any lawman riding for the federal government or a Union state was lower than a greaser with the clap, and they didn't hesitate to say so.

But Longarm wasn't calling on the Ranger captain, whom his own boss had already wired, because he was afraid some Ranger might insult him. He got along with some Rangers, and wasn't afraid of the silly ones. He simply didn't want any local Rangers appearing to recognize him, no matter how they felt about a federal lawman working in secret.

The old-timer Longarm met with in private had known Marshal Billy Vail of old, when they'd both been young squirts riding under Big Foot Wallace before the war, and he allowed he held no grudge against old Billy for siding with the Union and winding up a federal marshal once the dust had settled. He said he'd pass the word that no Ranger who'd ever met the famous Longarm was allowed to meet him in public again until further notice.

In return, Longarm naturally had to confide some of the suspicions about their local bail-bonding Triple 6.

The old Ranger leaned back in his swivel chair and opined, "Billy Vail used to worry more than the rest of us about horse shit too. I swear, I once saw him dismount to bust open and sniff a day-old turd he spotted on the trail."

Longarm quietly said, "Billy told me that tale. He got a citation for sniffing that horse turd. The horse that had dropped it had been eating oats, and you all were on the trail of Mexican border raiders, who feed their ponies cracked corn and encourage them to browse on any chaparral that ain't too thorny."

The older man grimaced and said, "All right, he convinced our patrol leader we were following the wrong trail. But *I* was the one who cut the right trail a day later and shot the leader of the Mex band personal. My point is that Billy Vail is suspicious by nature, and I fear he's sent you on a wild-goose chase. Us Rangers have already looked into them Triple 6 holdings. It's a big mishmash of family-owned-and-run businesses, inclined to back one another and use the old family brand, but otherwise independent. They got more than one cattle spread, a cotton spread with cotton gins, a wagon-freight company, that bail-bonding operation over to Courthouse

Square, and even a bookshop run by a priss of the family. The Wedfords have been here along the Trinity since nobody but Indians pissed in it. Ain't no Wedford ever been accused of stealing stock, cheating at cards, or riding for the North.''

He locked his fingers behind the nape of his neck to continue in an expansive tone. "The Wedfords are what we call *quality* in Texas. We got them inquiries from suspicious North Range jurisdictions, and as much as they pissed me, I had my boys investigate every case.''

Longarm nodded. "You'd have said so if they'd found anything.''

The old-timer unlocked his fingers and sat upright as he growled, "Damned right! When they let us establish the Texas Rangers again, we all took the same oath to the United States of America and its laws as underwrit by its ratified Constitution. I ain't sayin we cotton to each and every notion out of Washington. But we gave our word, and a good Texican would fuck his mother before he'd break his word.''

Longarm said soothingly, "Nobody's accused the Rangers of aiding or abetting any federal crimes.''

The Ranger captain snapped, "They've as much as called us foot-draggers or total idjets. We've gone over all them shootings by Triple 6 recovery riders. Lawmen in other parts where the shootings happened know better than us whether any charges could be brung at that end. We can only look tight at this end, and we have. Better than nine out of ten of the folks bailed out until it's time for them to stand trial have just come in to stand trial, and *their* bail money has been handed back, whether they beat the rap or not.''

He made a wry face. "None of *them* folks had to be tracked down by recovery riders. Of the ones who *did,* it's true more than half have wound up dead. But consider who we're talking about. How many sweet sissy boys get arrested and charged with anything to begin with? Bail bondsmen by definition are asked to go the bail of wilder sorts who've been rightly or wrongly established as trouble. It only stands to reason that any man who's been bailed out of jail after getting in trouble is looking for more trouble if he skips out on the contract he read and signed, waiving all his usual rights as provided by the Constitution for your average crook.''

He drew a fifth of bourbon from a desk drawer as he went on. ''The Wedfords play marbles for keeps, and the hardcases who skip out on any bail posted by the extended clan know it, or ought to know it. Judge Parker up to Fort Smith implied a poor innocent lamb gunned down in the Indian Territory had told his Black Seminole squaw he'd been framed. That may have been so. It happens. But there's no way a bail bondsman can frame anybody. He's only called in after the arrest and a hearing before the judge, who sets a date for the trial and only then decides how much bail to impose. So, as I wired Judge Parker my ownself, are we supposed to assume the Triple 6 recovery riders have been recruiting crooks to get arrested so's they can jump bail so's the Triple 6 recovery riders can track them down and shoot it out with them?''

He uncorked the bottle and held it out to Longarm as he demanded, ''What for? Target practice? Luke Cahill, the Caddo Kid, just got his fool self killed up in Dodge going after such an innocent lamb. When a man takes it into his head to jump bail, he's already primed for a serious discussion with the rider they are certain to send after him. So what's so sinister about our cut-and-dried courthouse gang's rough and ready, but perfectly legal ways, of doing business?''

''Their rough and ready way of doing business,'' Longarm replied as he raised the bottle to his lips. He took a swig, wheezed, and added, ''Good stuff. Triple 6 kills more bail-jumpers than any other outfit we know of, and more than one of the fugitives they'd killed weren't behaving as if they knew they were on the run. More than one managed to leave word they'd sure thought they were innocent, and it's possible to forge a man's signature to a bail bondsman's contract.''

The Ranger captain took his bottle back as he insisted. ''To what end and for what reason? I told you I'd had my own boys look into it. I can't say how many times *you've* been arrested, but take my word for the way it's done here in Dallas

County. At the risk of repeating myself, nobody from your bail bondsman is there, or has a lick to say, when others entire arrest you. It's only *after* you've been arrested, spent hours in a holding cell, and appeared for a hearing in front of the magistrate, who accepts a plea or remands you to a higher court for trial, that any *mention* is made of your damned bail.

"Once bail has been set, you and the bondsman appear before the court clerk and he approves your contract before he accepts the money and sets you free until you're supposed to come back. So are you suggesting some monstrous conspiracy betwixt Dallas County and the Triple 6 outfit? Are you asking us to buy the different court clerks whose names show up on different bail contracts are all in cahoots to frame innocent lambs with prior records by charging them with things that just never happened so's they could forge names to pointless bail papers and—"

"You're right," Longarm said, cutting in. "It's too complicated, and the jails of this fair land are filled with innocent lambs who were framed." He waved off a second offer of that hundred-proof red-eye as he rose and said, "I'd like to. I'd better not. I'd as soon have my wits about me as I close in on the outfit with some papers of my own to deliver."

The older man got to his own feet, saying, "Watch your step. You ain't backed by any badge or halfway reasonable story. So there's no saying how an outfit known to be rough and ready might respond to a vaguely sinister young man with a rep for shooting children."

Longarm grimaced and said, "I'm hoping they might consider the quick trigger finger of the late Crossdraw Culpepper a job qualification. I got one last question about that extended Wedford clan you seem to know so much about. There seems to be some sort of colored voodoo angle to more than one killing over mighty low bail. You said the Wedfords had been here in the Trinity Valley, raising cotton as well as cows, back in the times of the Peculiar Institution?"

The old-time Texican nodded easily and said, "Lord, yes, they had a whole lot of coons working for them. Free as well as indentured, on horseback and out between the cotton rows, with house niggers way too proud to associate with Mexicans. Most of them stayed on after the war and Mr. Lincoln's proclamation. Like I said, the Wedfords are *quality* who've always treated all their help right. But *voodoo,* that Creole crap with lots of screwing chickens and cutting young gals' throats? I'm pretty sure the Wedfords and all their help are either Baptists or Methodists. Mayhaps some of their Mex *vaqueros* are Papist, but I doubt you'll find one voodoo drummer on their payroll. You say you think some of the bail-jumpers who got shot were messing around with superstitious darkies?''

Longarm replied, ''Enough of 'em were to make you wonder. I've yet to hear of Frank, Jesse, or Billy the Kid puffing goofer dust at anybody. The quick and easy answer would be that the Wedfords have some colored help who know colored help all over the land. A heap of freemen of color were working on the railroads from hither to yon before the war. So there's at least a small colored quarter in every railroad town, and the Pullman porters have a sort of underground trade union that keeps them all in touch. But once we figure those white Triple 6 recovery riders are using some such misty grapevine, we're stuck with your observation that not too many white bail-jumpers have much call to keep in touch with colored folks from back home. It's sort of spooky when you study on it, even when you leave out grigri charms and goofer dust.''

They went out front to shake and part friendly. Longarm circled the stockyards to make sure nobody was tailing him. Then he ambled on over to the courthouse square and found his way to the upstairs offices of the Triple 6 Bonding and Finance Company.

He went in to find a smoldering copper-haired gal with new-penny eyes and that oddly orange complexion he'd seen before holding down the front desk. He told her he was Nero Culpepper, down from Dodge with some papers the late Luke Cahill had asked him to deliver.

She said to stay put as she rose to go in the back and an-

nounce him. She looked almost as pretty from behind. Longarm felt a stirring in his loins as he fondly recalled the last
time he'd met up with a gal with that coloring all over. She'd
been high-toned Spanish, and when he'd asked if all the gals
in Old Spain had copper pubic hair, she'd confided that only
the gals from one particular part of Spain where they grew
olives and fairy-tale castles seemed to share that peculiar coloring. There was another breed of high-toned Spanish gal who
had a longer face and sort of greenish ivory complexion, and
most of *them* were great in bed too.

The rounder-faced copper-haired gal came back, looking a
tad more friendly as she trilled, "I'll show you the way.
They've been expecting you, Mr. Culpepper."

"They?" asked Longarm with a puzzled smile.

To which she answered easily, "Mr. Wedford and the head
of our recovery department, Mr. Legrange. You probably
know him as Lash Legrange. He says he knows you on sight
if not personally. So Mr. Wedford said to bring you right on
back with me and then go down to the corner for some birch
beer because they want to talk to you in private."

# Chapter 10

It wasn't too late to run for it. He could drop the papers on her desk, make mention of others he'd forgotten, then make it down the stairs and around the corner before they got to wondering and came out to see what was keeping them.

Longarm took a deep breath, let half of it out so his voice wouldn't crack, and told her to just show him in. So she did. It felt like no more than a hop, skip, and jump before she was showing him into an office with a window overlooking the square. There sat a beefy cuss with a drinker's face, and a sort of reptile dressed in silver-trimmed black leather with an ivory-gripped Griswald .50-50 Conversion riding in a shoulder rig under his concho-trimmed *charro* jacket. Longarm wasn't surprised to have the gal introduce the beefy one in a business suit as Mr. Sam Wedford. The swarthy cuss in black leather had to be Lash Legrange. That awesome horse pistol he was packing had been produced with lethal effect in mind by an Atlanta jeweler named Griswald for Confederate cavalry officers as a cap-and-ball revolver. The newer cylinder chambered to load modern brass cartridges hadn't made the finely crafted and hand-fitted side arm throw any shorter. Longarm knew old Lash could drop most other pistol shooters while he was well out of their range, and at the moment they weren't three yards from one another.

So Longarm was about to explain who he really was and mention the recent visit to the Rangers when Lash Legrange nodded and muttered, "Yep. That's Crossdraw Culpepper, all right."

Sam Wedford smiled up at Longarm, saying, "It's nice to know for certain. Had us a Pinkerton man showing up a while back with some tall tale about being a former Frisco Vigilante looking to hire on as a recovery rider. You told Felicidad out front you knew the Caddo Kid and had some papers he gave you?"

Longarm hauled the folded sheaf from a hip pocket as he replied, "His real name was Luke Cahill and he never gave me these direct. When I heard he'd been shot, I went to the County Hospital in Dodge to see if there was anything I could do for him. He was in poor shape. To tell the pure truth, I ain't sure he knew who I was. But he groaned something this nurse followed better, and she was the one who took all this wilted and travel worn paper from a drawer and handed them over to me. It was my own grand notion to ask them for a copy of his death certificate. I figured you'd want that as well."

Longarm noticed the gal they called Felicidad had gone to get her birch beer. It left him feeling sort of lonesome as the two men stared thoughtfully up at him.

Sam Wedford handed the death certificate to Legrange, and went over the deliberately messed-up copies of Cahill's original papers on the late Gaston Dumas in Denver and Chuck Taylor in Dodge before he told Longarm, "You did better than Lash here. They told him he couldn't have anything but his own copy of Cahill's death certificate."

Lash Legrange nodded soberly and said, "That sheriff's deputy, Will Connors, lied to get out of admitting they didn't *have* those bail contracts. He likely didn't know Cahill had been packing them until I asked for them."

Sam Wedford explained, "Lash was there when Cahill and Taylor shot it out and killed each other."

The swarthy Legrange shook his head, flat Spanish hat and

all, objecting, "I was in Dodge. I wasn't with Cahill in that alley when he met Taylor. Things might have been different if I had been. I was at the Manhattan House, in bed with a friend, when I got word Cahill had been shot. You're so right about the bad shape he was in when I got to that hospital. I don't know why that nurse gave you and not me his papers. I told her I was a pal of his. But what's done is done, and I sure beat you down to Dallas by express wagon with the body, didn't I?"

Longarm smiled sheepishly and said, "You sure did. I never had no wagon freight outfit at my disposal, and it sure takes a while to work your way down here by rail. You say we were both at the Manhattan House at the same time, Mr. Legrange?"

Legrange said, "Call me Lash. I didn't know who you were the first few times I passed you in the lobby or watched you having a sort of spooky dinner in their dining room. I only paid attention to you after you shot it out with that mean-ass Simon Fuller out front."

Longarm nodded in sudden understanding, and replied in an easier tone, "I wasn't paying as much attention to the crowd gathered around as I was the town and county law."

Lash Legrange smiled knowingly and said, "We've all been in the same dumb situation after a gunfight. I didn't know at the time you were another old pal of the Caddo Kid. I had no dog in the fight out front of the Manhattan House. So I just watched that sheriff's deputy lead you away, and then I went about my own beeswax. I didn't know till Felicidad told us just now that you'd left town with them bail-bond contracts."

Sam Wedford tossed the papers Logarm had delivered to one side and declared, "We have our own carbon copies on file, and I'll have old Felicidad put these away as soon as she gets back. What are you saying we owe you for your trouble, Crossdraw?"

Longarm had never given Felicidad his fake nick name. So he knew they knew the full handle and rep of the real Crossdraw Culpepper. Legrange had doubtless asked around Dodge after the shootout with the late Simon Fuller.

Longarm said, "My friends just call me Cross, and you don't owe me toad squat, Mr. Wedford. The Caddo Kid asked me to see that you got his hunting licenses, and I figured as long as I was carrying them to you I'd bring along a copy of his death certificate. It only cost me four bits at the Ford County Coroner's office. So, seeing I've done what I came to do, I'll just move it on down the road and it's been nice talking to you."

As he started to turn toward the door, Sam Wedford blinked owlishly and said, "Hold on. You came all the way down from Dodge with Cahill's contracts and you don't expect anything for your trouble?"

Longarm shrugged and said, "It wasn't all that much trouble. I was on my way to Big D in any case and, like I said, the Caddo Kid and me went back a ways."

Lash Legrange decided, "He wants Cahill's job. He's just too shy to come right out and say so."

Sam Wexford asked, "Is that right, ah, Cross? The Caddo Kid told you we might hire you and that .44-40 if you dropped by with these papers he was packing?"

Longarm shook his head and replied, "Like I said, I could barely make out what he was saying. It was that nurse as told me he wanted you to get them papers. I confess I read through them on the train. I didn't have anything left to read after I'd finished all the magazines I'd bought off the candy butcher before dark. Reading the contracts you make clients sign gave me a better grasp on how come the Caddo Kid and Chuck Taylor wound up killing one another. But to tell the truth, enforcing such paper ain't my cup of tea."

He smiled with false modesty and added, "I'm a bounty hunter. I was one of the best before I got in trouble with the law over an innocent bystander and I mean to be the best again. I got my own fish to fry with a cut-and-dried warrant on a certain California road agent wanted by Wells Fargo. The warrant don't say dead or alive in so many words. But he's worth the same five hundred in the flesh or as another death certificate.''

Lash Legrange asked mildly who they were talking about. Longarm had chosen a real name that might just work with the same care with which he'd chosen the identity of a known bounty hunter nobody had seen running loose for some time. He hesitated, then said, ''Well, it's neither a lick of your beeswax nor a military secret. I'm tracking Big Thumb Gatewood, the terror of El Camino Real. I'd heard he was in Dodge. That side issue I got into with a loco trail boss had nothing to do with Gatewood's stage robberies out on the West Coast. I still don't know what Simon Fuller thought he had against me.''

Legrange said, ''I heard around town that some lady had hired you to gun him for gunning her husband.''

Longarm smiled thinly and said, ''I heard that too. I was after Big Thumb Gatewood. I'd just heard he'd been seen down this way by other Texas trail herders when Fuller called me out front of our hotel with results you know. I don't know whether Gatewood's really here in Big D, or any other part of Texas. But I don't know where else to look for him. So I'd best get on with looking for him in other parts of town.''

Sam Wedford started to say they paid less but could keep a gunhand busy. But Lash Legrange stopped him with a warning look, and neither tried to stop Longarm as he sashayed out of the room and through the now-empty outer office trying not to smile. Playing a five-pound rainbow or a copper-haired gal on a delicate trout line would likely take as much finesse, but he was after bigger fish and had to let them have as long a run as they wanted with his bait. He'd already seen they had something to hide. An honest bail bondsman with nothing to hide would neither send his gal at the front desk out in the street to play, nor hesitate to fill a vacancy with a known man hunter.

He glanced about for a soda shop as he left the building. But he didn't see any. So he asked a delivery boy on a pony for directions, and headed for the Cotton Exchange a quarter mile off.

He didn't want to buy any cotton. He was looking for the Red Mill Dance Hall. He found it with no trouble and, seeing the side door was open, went inside.

They weren't open for business that early in the day. The cavernous interior smelled of floor wax and stale sweat. Somewhere in the gloom a piano was idly tinkling, as if somebody was picking out a new sheet-music tune with one finger. A husky-looking gent with a German-silver mail-order badge pinned to his wilted shirtfront came out of the dim light and declared, "We don't open until after four and we ain't buying nothing, pilgrim."

Longarm said, "I don't want to dance with you and I ain't selling nothing. The name is Culpepper, Nero Culpepper, and I'm buying. I'll bet you a dollar you can't tell me anything about a trail herder by the name of Charles Edward Taylor who got in some sort of trouble in here a spell back."

The dance hall bouncer held out his hand and said, "You lose. I was the one who called the law."

Longarm asked how come as he handed a silver cartwheel over. The bouncer made it vanish as he replied, "Mean drunk who refused to check his gun at the door. They'd just told me that, and I was already on the way over, when he suddenly let fly at the floorboards and boots of a customer who swore he'd done nothing to deserve such rudeness. I let him empty his pissoliver before I threw down on him with my own and sent a runner for the precinct house around the corner. It was all over in little more time than it takes to tell. While we waited for the law, I asked young Taylor why he'd picked on that particular gent. He just grinned silly and said he'd admired the tooled Justin boots the cuss had on. His victim claimed, and others backed him, that he'd never seen Taylor before. The copper badges came and carried Taylor away and that was the end of it. Do you know how much time they gave him on the county roads?"

Longarm said, "He jumped bail. We are talking about a fairly clean-cut-looking kid in his twenties, trying to grow a mustache that would have been light brown if there'd been more of it?"

The bouncer shrugged and said, "Close enough. It ain't like we take photographs of every mean drunk we get in here of an evening. If it wasn't him, who was it? You say he made bail, then skipped out?"

Longarm grimaced and said, "That's about the size of it. Skipped on a hundred-dollar bail and, like you said, some possible time on the county road. A rider for the bail bondsman caught up with him a few days back in Dodge and that was it for both of 'em."

The bouncer whistled softly and said, "I was smart to wait until he'd emptied his wheel into the flooring! I knew he was mean, but I didn't know he was *crazy* mean! How come you're looking for him now that he's dead?"

Longarm made a quick excuse about family members feeling as confused about the ways of a mean drunk, and added, "He was living with what might have been a lady of color in Dodge. Is it safe to assume you never saw him dancing with anyone like that here at the Red Mill?"

"Dancing with a colored gal on *this* dance floor?" the Texican marveled. He shook his head and firmly declared, "Colored folks out for a good time don't come around this part of town after dark if they know what's good for 'em. The gals young Taylor was pestering in this dance hall were white as you or me."

Longarm thanked him for such light as he'd shed on the trouble Chuck Taylor had gotten into, and turned away, feeling pleased with himself so far. It stood to reason a bounty hunter who'd had a pal killed by Chuck Taylor would be curious about the young cuss.

He'd made it to the side door leading out to the sunny street when an all-too-familiar voice trilled out from the gloom, "Custis Long, you skirt-chasing rascal! What brings you down from Denver, and who told you I was working here, you sly dog?"

# Chapter 11

Longarm kissed her to shut her mouth, hauled her out the side door, and moved her along the brick wall to where it was safer to let her breathe before he let go. The white-hot steel sun in the cobalt-blue sky was cruel to the dark roots of her henna-rinsed hair, but otherwise Miss Red Robin was holding up well despite the life she led. He could see by the blue denim French smock that artists and show folk wore to rehearse in that she'd been the one plunking on that piano in the back. Red Robin played for the public in a red velveteen gown that set her curves off better. He had to take her curves on faith or by feel as she gasped, "Whoosh! You really must have been missing me, Custis!"

He put a gently firm finger to her lush lips and warned her in a whisper, "I ain't named Custis Long just now. I'd be Nero Culpepper, better known as Crossdraw Culpepper, the notorious bounty hunter."

Red Robin said, "If you say so, stud of my heart. You can tell me why you're working in secret after I show you *my* secrets at your place or mine. I'm staying at the Eagle's Nest Hotel if you'd care to join me at siesta time. I can't leave just yet. They say they want me to get that dance tune right, the fussy things."

Longarm said, "The Eagle Nest's too close to the center of

things here in Dallas. I checked into the Travis Hotel a couple of streets over with that in mind. I'm in Room 3-B, and I'd as soon you didn't ask at the desk."

She said she knew how to sneak in and out of hotel rooms. He knew this was the simple truth. He'd snuck into more than one hotel with her since first they'd met up in the Panhandle, when she'd been on the run after shooting that man who'd done her wrong in Chicago.

He'd been glad to discover the son of a bitch had lived. It was a pain to run in a gal you'd been intimate with, and Red Robin just loved to get intimate. The rest of the time she played piano, and it was sort of a shame she couldn't play piano half as well as she screwed. For she'd have been playing in great concert halls back East instead of roaming the West playing as best as she could.

On the other hand, had she screwed as poorly as she played the piano, they might never have gotten to be such pals. Like him, Red Robin liked to screw, and made no mush-bones about it when the time came to move on. So he knew it was safer to just give her his room number and trust to her common sense, rather than risk the fury of a Red Robin scorned and asking all over town for him.

She said she had to go back inside unless he wanted to risk meeting her boss out there. So he kissed her again and repeated what he'd said about not being in town as U.S. Deputy Marshal Custis Long.

When she ducked back in, he went his way wishing he hadn't met up with her. He knew he could trust old Red Robin as well as a man could trust most women. But as they said, the three fastest forms of communication were telegraph, telephone, and tell-a-woman. So he knew he'd have been safer if Red Robin wasn't in town. On the other hand, he was suddenly looking forward to La Siesta.

A plot of the early Texican folks had hailed from the Old South, where they'd already taken to "withdrawing" during the hotter parts of a Dixie day. So they'd adopted the Spanish custom of La Siesta as only natural, and "withdrew" formally between high noon, the *sexta hora* or sixth hour after dawn, and four in the afternoon, when things started to cool down tolerably. Folks from other parts who tried to *work* during the hottest hours of a Southwest day generally agreed, upon recovery, that there was a lot of sense in breaking both one's workday and time off into more sensible halves. Mexicans tended to work harder than Anglos in the Southwest, no matter what you heard, and made up for the lazy afternoons with shops and dance halls that stayed open past midnight. Then everybody went to bed late, got up at early cock-crow, and worked hard as they needed to until noon, when they all went back to bed, alone or with a bedmate of one's choice. They usually got their serious sleeping in while it was dark outside. The sultry shadows of shuttered windows during La Siesta could get sort of romantic when it wasn't too blamed hot.

So Longarm spent an hour at the public library, boning up on privately printed histories of Dallas families of quality, and headed back to his hotel, where sure enough, they'd locked up the dining room and the street entrance of the taproom for La Siesta as observed by Anglo Texicans, who never gave up drinking entirely.

Longarm went up to his third-floor corner room, and let himself in to find the maid had already closed the shutters and roller shades to hold in what was left of the morning coolness against the blazing sunshine outside. Longarm had chosen a room facing north and east with Texican sunshine in mind. So it wasn't too warm in the dimly lit room as he shucked his duds and treated himself to a whore bath at the washstand. He didn't need the wipe-down with a cool damp rag because it was that hot. He was expecting company. So he splashed on some bay rum from a saddlebag while he was at it.

Then there was nothing better to do than lounge atop the bedcovers in the nude and smoke a cheroot as he wondered what could be keeping old Red Robin.

He'd smoked the cheroot halfway down when he heard the soft, shy knocking on his door. So he swung his bare feet to the rug, rose in all his bare glory to step over to the door, and

83

swung it open to haul her in, lest someone out in the hall notice his full erection.

He hugged her tight for a friendly kiss as he swung her sweet rump to face the bed and kicked the door shut with a bare heel. He had her down across the bedding with his free hand up under her skirts as she twisted her face to one side and gasped, "Have you gone mad, good sir?"

That was when he recalled Red Robin shaved her snatch, and had to wonder whose hairy crotch he was petting in such a friendly way. So he rolled half off for a better look in the dim light, and felt mighty silly as he was forced to say, "I'm right sorry, Miss Felicidad. For a moment there, I thought you were somebody else!"

The copper-haired gal from the bail-bonding outfit tried to cross her bare thighs as she replied calmly, considering, "That seems obvious. Would you mind unhanding my private parts now, sir?"

Longarm hauled the two fingers out of her, and politely smoothed some no-doubt copper-colored hair back in place as he repeated his awkward apology and added, "If that ain't why you came here, is there anything else I can do for you, Miss Felicidad?"

She said, "Yes. To begin with, let me up, and would you please put something over your rather obvious manhood? I find it distracting to have a conversation in this ridiculous position!"

Longarm sat up and put a pillow in his lap as he asked her what she wanted to talk about. Red Robin was likely to find it distracting, and she was overdue already.

Felicidad sat up and primly smoothed her skirts down, murmuring to herself about something her mother had always told her about wearing undergarments no matter how hot it got. Longarm said he'd been the one in the wrong, and repeated his question as to what had brought her there.

Felicidad said, "I wanted to ask you about those papers you gave Mr. Wedford this morning. You say they were given to you by our recovery rider, Luke Cahill?"

Longarm shook his head and said, "Nope. I said a nurse handed 'em to me and said the poor cuss wanted me to deliver 'em. Is anything missing? I ain't never fiddled with bail-bond papers. So I'd be the last to know if there was anything wrong with 'em."

She sat silently beside him in pensive thought. So he asked her, "What's wrong with 'em?"

She said, "The papers on both Gaston Dumas and Charles Edward Taylor are made out in the same handwriting on standard forms. Can you account for that?"

Longarm could have. Unable to keep the originals held by the Ford County Coroner as material evidence, he'd asked for certified copies and then asked them not to certify them, so he could crumple them some without any embossed notary seals in hopes nobody would notice. Since somebody had, he shrugged his bare shoulders and replied in a desperately casual voice, "Beats me. I never filled out none of 'em. Like I said, I wouldn't know how."

Once again she sat in silent thought. So he asked, "What's so suspicious about the same Dallas court papers being writ by the same hand?"

She said, "They couldn't have been. Bond was set by different judges on different dates. So different court clerks made those papers out, and the bail *contracts* signed by two different clients were made out by our own courthouse runner, Howard Brinks. So how would you account for all the block print filling in the blanks and the signatures of two court clerks, two clients, and our own Howard Brinks written in the same hand?"

Longarm could only truthfully reply, "I never signed anything on any of those papers, Miss Felicidad. I follow your drift. But let me ask you another. What profit would there be for anyone in forging a recovery rider's hunting permits? Are you suggesting he had no call to gun either of those bail-jumpers, Dumas or Taylor?"

She said, "Of course not. They'd both jumped bail on us."

So Longarm said, "There you go. Your recovery rider was

in the right and the papers he was packing said so, no matter who writ 'em. So I don't see what's eating you, no offense."

She insisted, "I told you. They're blatant forgeries. Nobody here in Dallas filled out or signed any of then!"

He said, "Try her this way. The ones I got in Dodge had been soaked and dried out crinkle-crackle. Lord knows where old Cahill had been with them in his pants. What if he got caught in a gully-washer or had to wade a creek with the originals, had them copied on fresh forms, and gone on to get 'em wet some more before that nurse handed them to me up in Dodge?"

She demanded, "How and why would he have been swimming around on the High Plains in late spring to soak two separate sets of papers?"

Longarm replied more easily, "I don't have the least notion. I wasn't there. I'd suggest you ask him yourself, but we both know why you can't."

He rose to his feet in the gloom, still naked but holding the pillow over his old organ-grinder as he continued. "This mystery sure sounds interesting, Miss Felicidad. But it ain't my row to hoe and I've told you I was expecting other company, so . . ."

She got to her own feet. He couldn't tell in such light whether she was blushing or not. She sounded as if she might be when she told him, "I haven't said anything about all this to Mr. Wedford."

Longarm put one hand on the doorknob as he replied with a puzzled smile, "I don't see why not. It makes no never-mind to me whether you think somebody fiddled with those papers. I just delivered 'em as I was asked to. I never asked nothing for them and nobody gave me squat for them."

She said, "Lash Legrange is sure you're going to be back to ask for a job."

Longarm tried not to sound disappointed as he replied, "I don't see what would make him think that. I told him I had my own fish to fry in these parts."

She said, "He says you just made that up about some California want called Gatewood. He says you were washed up as a bounty hunter once you were sent to prison because a man with a prison record has a hard time packing a gun with small-town lawmen. He says you'd be far better off on any company payroll than on your own, if you're who you say you are.''

A big gray cat got up to stretch and swish its fuzzy tail in the naked deputy's innards as he said in as jovial a tone as he could manage, ''First I'm a forger of documents that can't be cashed for a wooden nickel, and now I'm posing as an ex-convict to get ahead in this world, Miss Felicidad? I wish I had your imagination. I'd write me a book as long as *Ivanhoe*, only twice as exciting, and make more money than Sir Walter Scott!''

She moved closer in the romantic semi-darkness to confide, ''I don't care what your game is, Nero. I don't trust Lash Legrange, and anybody he's suspicious of has to be on my side. So what are you really doing down here in Dallas?''

He laughed incredulously and sincerely at the notion she took him for such an easy mark. But seeing she seemed willing, he kissed her some more and let the pillow fall to the floor between them as, this time, she kissed back with enthusiasm in the French style.

Then he spoiled it all by confiding, ''I'm Nero Culpepper. My friends call me Cross and I'm in Dallas because they tell me Big Thumb Gatewood might be. But if it would make you like me more to hear I'm really a Pinkerton Man after Lash Legrange for aiding and abetting Frank and Jesse, I'd be proud to tell you how I figured it all out, after we've spent some more time on yonder bedstead.''

She pulled away, or started to. Then she gasped, ''Good heavens, you don't have a stitch on and it's pointing right at me!''

So he opened the door and she ducked out in the hall, flustered or sore at him. It was hard to tell from the clucking noises she made as she fluttered off in the gloom.

Longarm chuckled fondly and shut the door as he muttered,

"Never send a girl to do a spy-woman's job, Lash. But you sure are starting to box me in! I don't see how in thunder I'm to get any closer to the Triple 6 operation, or that copper-haired temptation, thanks to your suspicious nature!"

Longarm turned from the door as he pondered why an honest gunhand for a legitimate bail bondsman would be so suspicious about anybody to begin with. Then he heard more tapping on the door, and turned to open it again, asking, "Forget something?"

It wasn't the copper-haired Felicidad. It was the henna-rinsed Red Robin, and she'd changed to one of her red dresses to go out. Only she had the red sateen draped over one bare arm as she strode in grandly wearing just her black stockings and red high-buttons, naked as a jay from her red garters up.

Tossing her dress across a chair near the bed, Red Robin calmly said, "I thought she'd never leave. I thought it better to wait outside in silence when I heard you entertaining company in here, you big horny moose!"

Then, as she stepped closer, she spied his raging erection in the tricky light, and grasped the situation with one hand as she put her other arm around him and crooned, "Never mind, Precious Prick. Momma can tell when you've been waiting up for her. So all is forgiven!"

# Chapter 12

As she led him by the dong to the delights she'd been planning atop the bedcovers, Longarm reflected that it sure was a caution how different two gals could get without either one of them being ugly. The covers still smelled of Felicidad as Red Robin shoved him down across them on his bare back and got on top to fork her silk-sheathed knees to either side of his rib cage and lower her smooth-shaven crotch to impale herself on the raging erection occasioned by another woman entirely.

Longarm hissed in pleasure as Red Robin took it to the roots in her totally different twat. Longarm knew it had to be totally different because no two twats were the same, Lord love 'em all, and he'd been in this one before. It sure felt swell to mingle the familiar with the unexpected. Back in Denver on more than one occasion after he and the brunette Billie had been at it a spell, he'd managed to keep going by picturing it in this shaven snatch of Red Robin or parting the ash-blond thatch of good old Kim Stover up in the Bitter Creek country. But he was enjoying Red Robin too much as Red Robin to imagine anyone else bouncing up and down on top with her firm breasts bobbing and her dyed hair swirling as she shook her head like a wet bird dog out to go back for more.

Knowing her passions of old, even though it all felt somehow new that afternoon, Longarm rolled her over on her back without letting it slip out, and proceeded to pound her to glory as she wrapped her shoes and stockings around his bare waist to hug him deeper and begged him to show her no mercy as she seemed bent on breaking his back.

But they both survived, and later, propped up on pillows to cuddle and share a cheroot, they compared notes on how much more of such passion they had to look forward to.

Red Robin said she was booked at the Red Mill for the coming weekend, but had to be thinking of moving on. He told her he just didn't know how long he'd be in Dallas or where he'd be going next. So she insisted he tell her why, and by the time she had it up for him again, he'd told her the whole tale, as far as he understood it, and explained why he had to be Crossdraw Culpepper until he had a better notion on what was going on.

He could tell Red Robin was interested when she suggested they go dog-style. As most couples learn by the end of their honeymoon, that was the best position for a couple who felt like carrying on a conversation while trying for casual coming. Longarm stood by the bed with his bare feet spread on the rug as he gripped her soft ample hips and watched himself sliding in and out while her rectum winked up at him in time with her vaginal contractions.

She had her head down with a cheek turned to the bedding as she asked how he meant to track down Big Thumb Gatewood in a strange town the size of Big D.

Thrusting away, Longarm replied, "I wouldn't know where to begin. We got a tip he'd been seen here in Dallas a week or more ago. He may be long gone. He may be laying low somewhere in town. I just used one logical reason for a bounty-hunting Crossdraw Culpepper to be here in the same neck of the woods as that Triple 6 outfit. I was hoping they'd want to replace the late Caddo Kid with a known man hunter. I told you about that clumsy attempt by their office gal. So I reckon I ain't fixing to get the job."

Red Robin arched her spine and crooned, "Ooh, she'd have been the one to confess anything you wanted if she'd gone this far as a temptress! You tried and failed, of course?''

Longarm thrust into her until his pubic hair was tickling her baby-smooth labia as he calmly replied, ''I might have, if I hadn't been expecting present company. How would it have looked if you'd come in to catch us going at it like this, for Pete's sake?''

Red Robin laughed and decided, ''As horny as I've been of late, I might have just joined you! I'll bet we could get the truth out of her if we got her likkered up and made it three in a boat!''

Longarm didn't know whether she was teasing or offering sincerely. A man could get in a whole lot of trouble when two gals decided to test him, although he didn't see how Red Robin could be in cahoots with old Felicidad.

But they paid him to be suspicious, and so he casually asked, as he ground it around in her the way she liked it, whether she'd ever met up with old Felicidad.

Red Robin said, ''I haven't even *seen* her face-to-face. When I heard you had company in here, I ducked around the corner out in the hall and waited until I heard her leave. What did she look like? Her name sounds Mex, and you say she's the office gal for an Anglo bail bondsman here?''

Longarm said, ''Texicans only call Mexicans greasers if they're part Indian and it shows. Miss Felicidad's pure white with copper-colored hair. If her Spanish name bespeaks any local history at all, she likely hails from one of the old Spanish Land Grant clans. A heap of *Sangre Azulos* or blue bloods, as such Spanish called themselves, sided with the Anglo Texicans during the Revolution against Mexico. They felt no more kinship to Santa Anna and his Mexican dictatorship than anyone else north of the Rio Bravo.''

''You seem really taken with your henna-rinsed greaser!'' Red Robin pouted as she bit down with her moist insides. It would have been rude to suggest it took one to know one, or that Felicidad's hair looked naturally reddish. So he just went on thrusting friendly as he said, ''I'm more worried about why they sent her than what she looks like. I fail to see the method in their madness. If they're up to something shady and don't want an outsider to catch 'em at it, all they'd need to do would be nothing. You don't hire a hand you ain't sure you can trust. You don't need to send spies out after him.''

Red Robin suggested, ''Maybe she really was playing her own game then. Didn't you say she told you she didn't trust Lash Legrange and wanted you to help her catch *him* at something?''

Longarm grimaced down at the lovely view and replied, ''I couldn't risk it. Her words made as much sense as a recruiting speech or as a tried-and-true trap as old as the hills. Do you recall how Miss Helen of Troy came out in the dark when all them Greeks were laying low in the Trojan Horse?''

Red Robin said, ''I wasn't there personally, but as I recall the Iliad, didn't Helen try to make sure nobody was hiding inside that big wooden horse by calling out to them like a pal?''

Longarm said, ''There you go. They just laid low till she went away, and then they came out in the middle of the night to take the fort. So my best bet with old Felicidad is to just lay low and say as little as possible.''

Red Robin moaned, ''Your best bet with *me* involves my ankles locked around the nape of your neck with two pillows under my ass, you big tease!''

So he withdrew, rolled her on her back, and they finished her way. Not that he had any objections. The thought of trying to satisfy Red Robin and any other gal at the same time was awesome to contemplate.

Naturally he tended to, once they'd climaxed and cuddled at the head of the bedstead again to catch their second wind as the darkness all around commenced to get more sultry. It was easy to forget the old Texas sun pounding against the window shutters from outside with its white-hot fists. As he pictured Felicidad kissing him French while Red Robin blew tunes on his French horn, he decided, ''My best bet either way would be to stay the hell away from those bail bondsmen and let them make the next move, if they've a mind to.''

"What if they don't have a mind to?" Red Robin asked. "You just said their best bet would be to ignore you until you went away."

He sighed and said, "Billy Vail don't want me to go away. He wants me to find out what's been going on down here."

Since he'd told the whole story to Red Robin, and Red Robin was more interested than some women in what he did when he wasn't doing them, she'd paid enough attention to ask, "Did you see any darkies hanging about that bail-bonding outfit, or the courthouse square across the way?"

He fumbled for a fresh cheroot from the bed table as he shook his head and said, "Nope. Colored folks with no chores to tend to are not allowed to hang around courthouse squares in *Colorado,* for that matter. Luke Cahill, or the Caddo Kid, told me the owlhoot riders he was after tended to hide out in the more disreputable parts of railroad towns, where colored folks *are* inclined to hang around, trying not to stand out where the lights are brighter. So he must have been getting those tips from colored folks he knew in similar Dallas neighborhoods. I doubt any colored porters, let alone voodoo *hungans,* would come calling at the office."

Red Robin blinked and demanded, "Voodoo *what*?"

Longarm explained, "A *hungan* is a voodoo priest. I read that in a library book. Cahill was using some of that voodoo mumbo jumbo to get folks who believe in it back in line. So he must have known some such gentlemen of color. Somebody'd given him or sold him a bag of goofer dust, a powerful obeah or magic charm. He told me he didn't believe in the stuff himself, but he must have known at least one powerful *hungan* here in Dallas."

Red Robin began to toy with his limp manhood as she idly asked him, "What's a *mambo* if a *hungan* is a voodoo priest? I thought the word was *mambo*."

Longarm blinked in surprise, but went on thumbing them a match-head alight as he replied, "*Mambo* is a female *hungan,* or priestess, if they had it right in that library book. Where in thunder did *you* learn about voodoo, honey?"

As he lit the cheroot, she fondled his dong and casually replied, "I heard some maids at my hotel talking about it. I try to get on the good side of the hired help in a strange town because it can save a stranger in town a whole lot of trouble to know the parts of town to avoid. I've found Indian help don't much care how any white town is run. Mexican help care, but don't always understand, while the colored help always know more about the white powers-that-be than most white folks suspect."

Longarm took a drag on the cheroot and put it to her lips as he observed, "I've found colored hostlers and hotel help a good source of such information if you treat 'em decent. It's always surprised me how white folks with all sorts of things to hide never seem to notice the colored help as they meet other men's wives on the sly or plan a train robbery in a back room, as if the colored helper clearing the empties from the table was a factory machine with neither eyes nor ears. You say the maids at your hotel were jawing about a voodoo *mambo* here in Dallas, honey?"

Red Robin removed the cheroot from her lips and tried to encircle his dawning erection with a smoke ring. When she missed, she laughed and said, "You're not allowed to attend. They were talking about some bamboo party they'd been invited to by this *Mambo Royal,* and from the way they were sniggering, it sounded like a lot of fun. But an artistic white girl has to draw the line somewhere. So I didn't ask when or where they were holding this bamboo party."

Longarm thought back to those books on the subject and asked Red Robin, "Are you sure they didn't call it a *banda* or a *bambouché?*"

She said, "Either sounds as sensible. What's the difference?"

Longarm explained, "A *banda* is a voodoo rite, involving lots of drumming, dancing, drinking, and screwing, whilst a *bambouché* is just a sort of church social involving lots of drumming, dancing, drinking, and screwing. Will you let go my cock whilst I'm talking to you, Miss Robin?"

She laughed wickedly and decided, "I mean to *bambouché* it some more. Do these voodoo-dancing darkies screw just anybody at those get-togethers, or can you bring your own partner?"

He truthfully replied, "I don't know. I've never been to either a *bamba* or a *bambouché*. You say those colored gals were talking about attending such a gathering in the future tense?"

Red Robin swore and demanded, "Don't you ever think about anything but solving mysteries when I'm spraining a wrist to get it back up for the both of us? Do it some more and forget those sassy colored girls at my hotel. Neither one of them is half as young or pretty as I am, and even if that wasn't so, I'll not have you rutting with total strangers of any size, shape, or color at a crazy voodoo dance!"

He snubbed out the cheroot and rolled between her wide-spread and welcoming thighs, knowing better than to waste precious grains of sand in the hourglass of one lifetime on needless arguments with women. Thus a good time was had by all, if they ignored how sweaty it got that last time with his hotel room warming up in spite of the shades and shutters. So once she'd come again, Red Robin suggested what she described as a "nappy poo" before he had to escort her back to her own hotel near the Red Mill.

He rolled off and sat up so she could lay panting, spread-eagled and damp, while he relit that cheroot, got his breath back, and rose to pour clean water over a washcloth at the corner stand. Then he wiped a lot of sweat and Red Robin off his own bare hide before he wrung the cloth out, wet it again, and carried it back to the bed for the well-laid Red Robin. She blessed him back to his grandfolks as she wiped her self down from her flushed face to smooth-shaven crotch.

He felt mildly surprised by the stirring in his own innards while he watched her do that. She'd told him when first they'd met that she shaved down yonder for sanitary reasons as she roamed a West lacking proper sanitary facilities along many a stretch. Longarm knew ticks could be a caution for someone crapping in an aspen grove off the trail. But he suspected her real reason was to hide the true color of her natural hair. Henna rinsing between the thighs sounded complicated as hell.

She asked if she might have a dry towel as well, to finish up her reclining refreshments. Longarm rose again to toss her a clean one, and she purred, "Oh, Lord, that feels almost as nice as screwing."

Then she thoughtfully added, "If I let you carry me back to my own hotel, you're not going to pester those colored maids about that wild and crazy voodoo affair they were talking about, are you?"

He flopped back down beside her, cheroot gripped in his grinning teeth, as he replied, "You have my word I won't say one word to any of the help at your hotel."

He knew that if the colored help at her hotel had heard about a big *bambouché* presided over by some royal voodoo queen, the colored help at *this* hotel would have heard about the same affair, and no matter what name he registered under, Longarm had always made a point of talking polite and tipping proper.

# Chapter 13

After he'd carried Red Robin back to her own hotel and returned to his own, Longarm hit pay dirt out back with the stable hand they called Calvin.

Calvin didn't believe in "that voodoo shit," until Longarm bet him a dollar he didn't know anything about that big *bambouché* he'd heard some ladies jawing about. As the grinning colored kid pocketed what amounted to more than his regular day-wage, he confided, "Ain't gwine be a good-times *bambouché*, Cap'n. Queen Esther holding a real *banda* at her *humfo* 'cross White Rock Creek after midnight when the law be in bed wiff they own Good Books."

Longarm bet him another dollar he didn't know how to get there.

Calvin stared down wistfully at the silver cartwheel in the white man's palm and said, "I be a born-agin Baptist, Cap'n. But s'pose you come back wiff you' saddle around elebben, I might have a member of La Societé Voudou willing to carry you along as a respectful guest. Ain't up to me to say how much you'll have to bet or whether the answer gwine be *oui* or *non*. I jess works here, and like I say, I don't *believe* in that Gulf Nigger shit."

So Longarm gave him the extra dollar anyhow, and they parted friendly. With half the hours of darkness to kill, Longarm prowled the underbelly of Dallas as the bright lights were lit after sundown to let the good times roll for Anglos, coloreds, Mexicans, and any Indians who knew how to act in town.

Most of the few Indians he passed on the lamplit streets on the wrong side of town looked to be Caddo, the large but almost forgotten nation that spoke the same lingo as the more famous Pawnee but hadn't acted as fringed and feathery. Like their Pawnee cousins, the Caddo had farmed along the bottomlands as hard as they'd hunted on the plains all around. They'd had as much trouble with the more ferocious Comanche as anyone else the Comanche could get at. So they'd welcomed armed and dangerous Anglo-Mex neighbors as a possible improvement on their neighborhood, and taken to more civilized farming and ranching notions like ducks to water. So the Anglo-Mex Texicans had found *them* one hell of an improvement over Comanche, Kiowa, Apache, and such, with the result that you had to look tight to tell a Caddo cowhand from a Mexican *vaquero* of late. You could usually bet on a dusky young hand in faded denims and a tall Texas hat being Caddo instead of Mexican because the Mexicans tended to dress more outlandishly.

Longarm wasn't looking to guess the ancestry of the loud and quiet gents he looked over in many a Dallas saloon and pool hall that night. He was looking for Big Thumb Gatewood, as long as he had the time to act out a dead bounty hunter's part. He knew the real Cross Culpepper would be nursing his drinks and drifting from bar to bar in the parts of town a stranger riding the owlhoot trail would tend to frequent.

As both bounty hunters and most lawmen knew, shady strangers in a new town felt safer in the parts of it they'd seen first and hadn't run into trouble in. It wasn't true they were safer closer to railroad depots or on the downtown streets where travelers passing through, or country folks in town to unload beef or produce, might be found. Outlaws who knew a town well enough to board in some much tamer part of it and drink sedately in respectable neighborhood saloons were really a bitch to track down, even when you'd been told they were in town.

But Big Thumb Gatewood didn't have known Texican kith or kin, and the feature that had earned him his nickname was another break for a sharp-eyed man hunter. Big Thumb Gatewood was said to keep his right hand in his pocket and pay for his drinks with his natural left hand. This was because the thumb of his right hand was more than twice the size it should have been. Whether he'd been born that way, or had had some accident to his right hand, depended on whom one asked. But there it was, and they said Big Thumb Gatewood used that oversized thumb on his gun hand in a wondrous manner.

Whatever he had wrong with his monstrous thumb, it functioned as a normally nimble but awesomely strong one. He packed a Schofield .45-28, side-draw and tied down when he was afoot. He had another brace of surplus army revolvers lashed to the swells of his saddle when he was out stopping stagecoaches. In either event, it appeared he'd filed the sears of his six-guns so that they revolved their wheels and fired with that big thumb alone cocking their hammers in a manner few natural thumbs could have managed.

One of the gunslicks Ned Buntline told of in his dime magazines had filed the sears of his single-action Colt so he could "fan" the hammer with his other hand. More than one aspiring border badman had gotten himself killed trying *that* wild notion. For aside from firing faster in a gunfight, it helped a lot if you could sort of keep your weapon *aimed* at the cuss firing back at you with bullets of his own.

They said Big Thumb Gatewood could hold his aim tolerably as he fired a single-action but accurate Schofield as fast as double-action with his freak gun hand. There was no mystery as to why he tried to keep the thumb out of sight when he wasn't fixing to draw on anybody. Big Thumb Gatewood had made it to the fifth grade of a little red schoolhouse in the Cumberlands before he'd had to leave home in a hurry for hitting his daddy back with a shovel. Anyone who could read at the fourth-grade level would know about those reward posters describing his peculiar gun hand.

Longarm noticed, as he moseyed about Downtown Dallas, that most of the Anglo gents he saw had their right hands going about their natural chores in the open air. Mexicans and Indians didn't count, though he didn't see many of either mooching about with their hands in their pockets on such a warm evening. There were no colored hands mooching about with their hands doing anything. There were colored cowhands in Texas. A lot of colored cowhands in Texas. But like colored cavalry or the better-paid Pullman porters and railroad depot porters, such gentlemen of color had their own saloons and houses of ill repute where a colored gent could act more naturally without some unreconstructed rebel like the late Clay Allison asking what he was grinning about.

The only white man Longarm saw with a right hand in his pocket who fit the description of Big Thumb Gatewood was packing his Dance Brothers revolver riding cross-draw. Longarm wasted the better part of an hour making dead certain that the California road agent hadn't switched to a more practical gun rig as well as a cheaper six-gun. It felt dumb to follow a stranger into the craphouse, but the half-drunk rider armed with a half-ass revolver had a regular hand when he took it out of his pocket to take a piss.

Having pissed in turn, and seeing it was getting on toward eleven, Longarm drifted back to the Travis Hotel, and fetched his borrowed stock saddle and regular bridle from his hired room. When he toted it out back to the hotel stable, he found Calvin there alone. But the friendly colored kid saddled a black gelding that rented for two bits and said he'd spoken to that member of La Societé Voudou. When he said the guide would be back from taking a leak directly, Longarm handed over the extra change and said, "Swell. How come your voodoo friends talk so much French if it's supposed to be an African notion?"

Calvin shrugged and said, "I told you I be Baptist, Cap'n. Darkies where I grew up, over on the Brazos, praise de Lawd in plain English. *Obeah, voudou,* whatever you wants to call it, started in the bayous of French Louisiana where Ofay Law not so strict 'bout uss'n after hours. Warn't no Black Codes in French Louisiana until the French slaves in Haiti scared them Creoles so. I reckon by that time so many white ladies had been taught to buy grigris and pay for *wangas* by they mammies, warn't nobody able to stomp out La Société. You won't be the only ofay 'tending Queen Esther's *banda* tonight, you see.''

Longarm knew what some colored folks meant by *ofay.* It didn't vex him to be called *Wasichu, Saltu,* and such by Indians. He'd never been ashamed of being a white man. He knew what a grigri was now, and he figured he'd wait and ask someone who *believed* in voodoo what the hell a *wanga* might be.

They'd led the black pony out in the moonlit paddock by the time his guide to the *banda* rites showed up, riding a mule bareback and astride to show a heap of dark thigh. Calvin hadn't told him the guide to the other side of midnight would be a gal of no more than sixteen in a frilly Mexican blouse and red fandango skirts with neither shoes nor any head covering, save for all those ribbons holding her woolly hair in stand-up tufts like the pictures of Topsy in *Uncle Tom's Cabin.*

Calvin introduced her as a Miss Chastity Grimes, and she ignored Longarm's polite hat-brim tick as she pouted, ''I wants sebben dollars an' I spect to be treated like a lady of quality at the *banda* 'cross the creek, hear?''

Longarm gravely replied, ''I don't see what's so tough about that, Miss Chastity. *Ain't* you a lady of quality?''

She softened a mite, but didn't smile as she said, ''Gimme the money and let's be off then. But remember, white boy, you s'posed to do as you' told once we get on Queen Esther's private property. This don't be no coon shoutin' in the cottonwoods with the Rangers coming to save you do you holler. Ofay law don't *'ply* where we gwine tonight. Be you willin' to do as you' told and learn, or be you wantin' to jess keep you' damn sebben dollars?''

101

Longarm handed her the fistful of silver and mounted up beside her as he soberly said, "I'd like to know more about your *wangas* and such, Miss Chastity."

So she neck-reined her mule back out on the alley, and grudgingly told him to come along. She waited until they were out of the alley and headed east toward the Trinity before she asked, "Who tell you so much about *wanga,* white boy? Calvin say you didn't know much about the grandmammy ways of the old woods of home."

Longarm honestly replied, "I don't. I read some library books on voodoo, *vodun,* or whatever you call it. No offense, but I had a tough time following the theology. When I heard there was some sort of Black Mass being held across the river tonight—"

"Bite you pink tongue, Ofay!" she cut in, blazing indignantly on. "That Black Mass shit be the silly notions of *your* kind! Ain't no debbil worship to our ways of evoking our own *loas,* see?"

He said, "I'm trying to. What's a *loa,* something like a haunt?"

The young but obviously devoted follower of the cult replied in a less certain tone, "*Loa* don't translate right when you try to 'splain it in Creole or English. You can call a *loa* a haunt, a spirit, a power, or a force, but 'lessen you talk the *grandmammy* talk, you ain't talking right about no *loa.*"

"Medicine," Longarm decided, going on to explain. "Indians arguing religion with me have had the same trouble explaining Wakan Tonka, or that Great Spirit white missionaries will go on about. The Lakota say Wakan translates as well, or as badly, into Medicine, Magic, Spirit, or just plain Mystery. Old Sitting Bull told me personally that when he cuts himself in honor of Wakan Tonka, he pictures Wakan Tonka as the one great mystery no mortal man will ever really understand."

She asked when he'd met Sitting Bull.

Remembering he was supposed to be Cross Culpepper, Longarm told her a big fib about looking for a wanted breed on a so-called Sioux agency. He doubted she'd be interested in the fine distinctions between the words Sioux, Dakota, and Lakota.

She said, "Don't say anything for a spell and don't call back when we get yelled at. We got to pass a crazy white lady's house along the road to the creek. But she's the only one on this street who sets on her veranda day and night."

Longarm knew the type, and followed the colored gal's drift just a few minutes later when a voice cackled at them from the darkness. "Who goes yonder at this hour? Stop right there and answer me or I'll have the law on you!"

When they were out of earshot, Chastity sighed and said, "I hopes I don't go crazy when I old and ugly. They say Queen Esther look the same now as she did when she be a play-pretty of General Andrew Jackson back in New Orleans. Queen Esther be a *mambo macombo* wiff *powers*!"

He'd read that phrase. He said, "You're talking a mighty big witch woman, right?"

The true believer sniffed and snapped, "Not the way you-all means witch woman. *Ofay* witch women s'posed to worship your ofay Debbil and kiss his asshole. We ain't got no one Lord or Debbil to pray or fear. We got *rada loas* that be good and *petro loas* that be bad. But most of our *loas* be good or bad depending who calls on them to do what, see?"

He confessed, "Not hardly. One of those books I mentioned held that your sort of folks in Haiti came up with voodoo, whilst others held in Cuba invented Santeria, and they called it Macombo in Brazil."

She said, "Shit, s'pose you 'splain to me the differences between Baptist, Congregationalist, or Methodist Protestants! How you gwine spell things the Grandmammies of the old ways said, when they didn't know how to read or write? *Santo* is the Spanish Creole for *loa,* and do you say it M'Cumba or Macombo, it still the Grandmammy way of saying big and powerful, see?"

He decided, "Sort of. This Biblical scholar I talked with on a long train ride one time held that *Salaam, Salem, Shalom,* and *Shiloh* were ways old-time writing with no vowels got rendered into our own. They writ it something like S.L.M. in the original Hebrew. And nobody's too sure whether to put down Dakota, Lakota, or Nakota, which may be why the BIA spells it Sioux. I reckon I'll just keep my mouth shut and listen with my ears open tonight.''

The dark route she'd chosen led between two abandoned buildings to shallow White Rock Creek, flowing like barely moving ink in the moonlight. Chastity reined in and produced something white from the folds of her fandango skirt as she warned, ''Before we cross over, we'd best get some rules of La Societé straight, white boy. Before we gets to *humfo,* we s'posed to put these flour-sack masks over our heads. Ofay law don't 'prove of some of our ways, and it ain't nobody's business who be there tonight.''

As he took the flour sack she added, ''When we gets there, the *hungans* or magician-priests gwine ask you to check you gunbelt and take off all you clothes. Queen Esther put a powerful *wanga* on anybody who'd steal at one of her *bandas.* So you'll get you shit back. But you got to 'tend the *banda* masked and bare-ass, like all the others, black, or white. Then you have to do as Queen Esther or her *hungans* tell you, no matter how it rubs you white ass the wrong way. Do they tell you to dance, you s'posed to dance. Do they tell you to fuck, you s'posed to fuck. If that be too rich for you blood, you'd best say so now and turn back, hear?''

Longarm gulped and said, ''We'd best go on, seeing we've come this far. Who are you expecting them to require me to rut with, Miss Chastity? Anyone I might already know?''

Chastity Grimes shrugged her dusky bare shoulders and replied in a demure tone, ''Maybe me. Maybe somebody else. Anyone you fucks at a *banda* gwine be masked and you ain't s'posed to let on you knows 'em whether you knows 'em or not. Queen Esther put a mighty mean *wanga* on anybody who reveals religious secrets, see?''

He nodded soberly and didn't ask for the exact translation of the word. *Wanga* had to mean something like *curse,* whether they believed in witchcraft as white folks thought of witchcraft, or as something worse.

# Chapter 14

Chastity had said the mysterious Queen Esther owned the property her *humfo* or voodoo temple sat on. She hadn't warned him what a tangled wood they were riding into. Second-growth saplings of alder, cottonwood, crack willow, and other bottomland weed trees had sprung up thickly on what seemed to be an abandoned cotton spread. The Spanish Creole-style plantation house was screened on all sides by the dense growth only possible where a heap of sunlight and a high water table combined to inspire vegetation to riot. In its glory days as a white-run cotton spread, they'd have kept the veranda railings wrapped around the main house clear and open to the Texas sky and breezes. You got enough mouse-sized roaches and meaner little chiggers without all that damp green cover smack against your quarters.

Longarm heard no drums and saw nobody screwing as they rode in a tad before midnight. As she'd warned him, the burly half-naked black gents who greeted them when she led the way around to a side corral told her white companion politely but firmly that neither side arms nor pants were allowed inside.

Fortunately, it was fairly dark, with the only light coming from the beclouded moon overhead and some candles set in the windows along the veranda as Longarm and Chastity got undressed. They'd put their fool flour-sack masks on before riding in.

Longarm was glad as they took everything else he'd had on and said they'd see he got them back when Queen Esther said it was time he got them. As warm as the night was, he felt goose fleshed by the time he was standing jay-naked next to a bare black gal with a white sack over her head. He hoped his fool pecker wouldn't rise to the occasion when she took him by the hand and led him inside.

He felt sillier inside. The main hall of the old run-down plantation house was crowded with stark-naked folks of various shapes and shades of color, with a surprisingly large number of fat naked white women. They were standing around chatting through their masks like early arrivals at a regular church waiting for the services to start.

The crowd of perhaps four score only seemed large until one thought about the size of the combined Fort Worth-Dallas settlement. For if no more than eighty made up the biggest voodoo cult in the Trinity Valley, only a tiny fraction of the population, Anglo, Mexican, or colored, believed in what Calvin at the hotel had described as "voodoo shit."

Longarm noticed Chastity had wandered off and left him standing there like a naked big-ass bird. Then another voice calmly asked if this was his first *banda*.

Longarm turned to find himself in the company of a stark-naked and well-built white gal wearing a black silk sack over *her* head. In the dim light he could see she had what seemed an upside-down Star of Texas dangling between her shapely bare tits on a thin gold chain. He tried not to look further down as he replied in a desperately calm voice that he'd never been to one of Queen Esther's services before.

The white gal chuckled and said the meaning of *Esther* seemed apt for a self-styled queen of an oppressed people. He said he'd heard the voodoo queen, or whoever, owned this run-down cotton spread gone to weed trees. The naked lady shrugged her bare shoulders and replied, "So they tell me. Cotton takes richer soil and cheaper labor than livestock. So

106

many an old Texas planter took to ranching once the Peculiar Institution ended. Are you here to write a book, buy a grigri, pay for a *wanga,* or just in hopes of changing your luck?''

Longarm laughed and parried, ''Ain't nobody offered to change my luck for me. Does it count when the offer's from a white gal?''

She didn't answer. A tall ebony *hungan,* or maybe just a waiter, came over, naked as a jay, with a tray of something black in brandy snifters. The white gal in the black mask told him, ''Have some rum and coca. You won't feel as naked and shy.''

He tasted the concoction. He could tell there was rum in it. Lord only knows what that *bitter* shit might be.

He turned to comment on the taste, but found the naked white gal in the black mask had vanished like a puff of smoke. He muttered, ''Once a prick-tease ever a prick-tease, with or without any duds on!''

He sipped more of the curious brew, not feeling any less naked or shy and dying for a smoke. Then another naked but masked gentleman of color sidled up to politely tell him he'd been granted an audience. So Longarm followed him, snifter in hand, wondering what that meant.

What it meant, once he'd followed the *hungan* up the stairs and on down a long cobwebbed hall to a room lit by a candle in a ruby tumbler, was an audience with a mighty spooky-looking gal indeed!

If it *was* a gal. The whatever seated on the far side of a small round table draped with a Spanish shawl seemed to be built like a woman under a Mother Hubbard of paisley-printed calico. Her hands were encased in white kid gloves that came clean to her elbows, and for some reason she had dried chickens' feet strung with bones and beads around her neck. But the hardest part to take was the papier-mâché skull with a carrot-red wig of wool yarn down to her shoulders and a stovepipe hat Abe Lincoln must have left on a train perched atop her skull-masked and red-wigged head.

She said, "Have a seat and tell me why you are so troubled, Ofay."

Longarm squatted on the hassock provided, wondering who else's bare ass had recently warmed the same leather as he replied, "I ain't feeling troubled, Queen Esther. You are Queen Esther, ain't you?"

The voodoo queen nodded her ghastly head gravely and said, "I am. You say you are Crossdraw Culpepper, a hunter of men who comes to us with a heavy heart because you are not who you say you are and because the man you say you are hunting is not really the reason you are here in Texas."

Longarm had once slept with a professional stage magician, and she'd told him the secrets of "cold reading" as they called it. So he just stared through the eyeholes of his mask at the mask of the voodoo queen and waited. Cold reading called for the mark to respond to the reader's first feelers. There were dozens of ways a halfway clever cold reader could have heard a bounty hunter called Crossdraw Culpepper was coming to her midnight gathering. That other magic gal had told of this spirit medium who'd blow into town ahead of time to go through the records at the county clerk's office before he turned up officially to hold a spirit-rapping party. Knowing things such as the names of dead grandparents, the address of that boyhood home on the far side of town, or how a favorite uncle had been killed in the war gave a fortune-teller an edge on the common sense of the average mark. Once a professional mind-reader hit low with things he or she shouldn't know about, the mark they were reading tended to spill more without knowing what he was spilling. Most of us tend to make ourselves out to be more than we really are. Everybody jerks off and has other dirty little secrets a cold reader could hint at to convince anybody with a guilty conscience that it's no use trying to hide the truth from anyone with such mystic powers.

Unless the mark just sits there, grinning, behind his flour sacking.

Queen Esther stared back from the skull holes of her own

mask for a long spooky time before she asked, "What *wanga* do you seek from me?"

Longarm shrugged his bare shoulders and said, "I never said I was in the market for any voodoo curses, no offense. Like I told the gal who brung me, I'd heard some other gals jawing about the mysterious voodoo rites going on out here at the old Wedford Plantation, and so I figured I'd come over the river and see what was going on."

"Who told you this property once belonged to the Wedford family?" Queen Esther asked, too quickly to have spent much study on it.

Longarm flat out lied. "This naked lady told me. I can't say I care who owns the property now. I'm a bounty hunter, not a real-estate man."

She said, "I knew that. What makes you think the man you seek may be hiding out among colored folk here in Texas?"

Longarm said, "He's hiding out somewhere. The Rangers ain't found him in the usual haunts of white strangers in town. It's known Henry McCarty, known as Billy the Kid, holes up with Mexican gals, whether he's an Irish kid from New York City or not. Owlhoot riders as white society don't approve of tend to hole up with other socially unaccepted folks, be they trash white, breeds, colored, Mex, or whatever. The road agent I heard was here in Dallas ain't of Texican Anglo background. He hails from the Cumberlands, where hardly anyone speaks Spanish. But he might get along better with colored folks than, say, Clay Allison or your average rider with the Ku Klux Klan."

"Then you were expecting to find him out here at this *banda*?" she demanded in what seemed a sincerely worried tone.

Longarm shook his head and said, "Not now that I've seen the mixed crowd you draw, Queen Esther. To begin with, the cuss I'm after tends to keep his right hand in his pants pocket, and nobody downstairs is allowed to wear pants."

Queen Esther sighed and asked, "Why do you keep lying to me? Don't you know I know who you really are?"

Longarm didn't bite. He said, "I am who I am and that's all that I am, ma'am. If I ain't welcome here, I'll just be on my way and we'll say no more about it, hear?"

She laughed inside her skull mask and said, "I know lawmen are not allowed to arrest anyone they've sacrificed to the *vodun loas* with."

Longarm laughed incredulously and asked, "Is that all that stands in our way, Queen Esther? Why don't you heist your skirts and I'll be proud to sacrifice a load in you this instant, odd as you may look in that fool mask and fright wig."

Queen Esther laughed lewdly and said, "Perhaps another time. I'm expecting other ofays with business of their own with me right now."

So Longarm rose, limp-dicked in spite of his brag, and allowed he could hardly wait as he turned away. Out in the hall he found others lined up: a colored man, two colored women, and a naked white gal who wouldn't look at him in spite of her own mask. It wouldn't have been polite to tell her lots of skinny gals had saggy tits. So he never did as he finished his drink and strode on by.

Downstairs, he found the party had commenced to liven up, with a reed pipe playing wicked tunes while somebody tapped a bongo drum softly but in time with the dog-style screwing of the couple in the center of the candlelit bare-floored room. The gal on her hands and knees was milk-white or freckled, depending on where the sunlight had been hitting her. The gent throwing the blocks to her from behind was black as ebony and shining with sweat as he grinned down at her pale rump, or seemed to, since he was also wearing a skull mask.

It was easier to see now why Queen Esther had her followers wear masks. Miscegenation wasn't only against the *law* in Texas. It tended to inspire Lynch Law, whether the white women were willing or not.

Longarm backed into a corner to observe from the shadows where his dawning erection might not show. He knew he was supposed to be shocked, but thanks to that drink, he suspected, the sight of a fat old white man going down on a masked colored gal built like Chastity Grimes had no discouraging effect on the raging erection he was having now.

He backed into a corner, feeling silly, while across the room a colored kid with an impossible dick was jacking it off shamelessly.

Then someone was jacking *him* off, and he was relieved to see it was that white gal in the black silk mask. She asked, "Were you saving all this for little old me?"

He gallantly replied he surely had been as he swung her sweaty bare breasts around to flatten against his chest and growled in her ear, "Why don't we step out on the veranda and get out of this dumb upright position?"

But even as she parted her pubic hair with the tip of the manhood she so firmly grasped, she insisted, "We're not supposed to sacrifice in private. Get dirty with me here and now!"

So he did, as most men would have, but had to ask as he entered her passionate depths whether she really considered this a *sacrifice*.

Moving her pelvis to meet his thrusts, she moaned, "In the beginning the *vodun loas* fucked night and day in the wind and rain to create all that *is*. Dambulo fucked Sogbo up the ass while Rainbow fucked Thunder to create Music. Fuck me now, to the beat of the drums, and see what magic *we* can make!" It felt dumb as hell, even by dim candlelight, but it felt mighty good as well, and nobody else really seemed interested. Then he spied the grotesque figure of Queen Esther staring down at everyone from her staircase with a crazy grin across that papier-mâché skull she had on. So he couldn't tell how much he might have rattled her with that lucky guess about the former owners, or likely the real owners, of this run-down cotton spread. The notion that any freed slave claiming immortality and magic powers would be granted a property deed on the tax rolls of any Texican county seemed mighty slim. It had made more sense that a powerfully connected white owner would be indulging the fancies of a family witch doctor.

Then he noticed he didn't seem to be screwing that nicely built gal with an inverted star between her breasts. The gal he was pounding into the hardwood floor was paler, skinnier, and had the same saggy tits as he'd seen in the hall upstairs. They looked more interesting with their big nipples swirling around in circles like that as he tried in vain to come while she sobbed, "Do it! Do it! Do it! Make the *loas* come out of the dark woods after the man who killed my Tommy!"

He didn't have the least notion who her Tommy was, or who *she* was, for that matter. There was a lot to be said for masked sex orgies in a town no bigger than Dallas.

She tried to kiss him through the sacking they both had on, with panting mouths agape. Then he lost track of what she was saying about her Tommy, for she'd turned into a bigger gal with prouder tits and a far darker complexion. She moaned that she was fixing to come. He never asked what she was doing there. He just kept thrusting in and out to no avail until he just had to roll off and find another glass of that rum and coca to wet his parched throat.

The bitter-sweet concoction hit the spot, and he was ready to go again with the wildest collection of sizes, shapes, and complexions he could imagine. There was no way of telling whether all or any of them were pretty, ugly, or in between. Most any gal felt pretty while you were sliding it into her for the first time.

After that he lost track of the time and space he was doing all sorts of things in, until he suddenly found himself staring up at a pressed-tin ceiling with all his duds back on. He had his wallet and his guns, but no memory of asking for them or that pony. He was pretty sure he'd somehow wound up back in his bedstead at the Travis Hotel with something that felt disgusting in one hand.

He raised his hand warily. By the dim light of the low trimmed lamp on the bed table he could see he held a dead chicken's dried-out claw. There seemed a note attached. It seemed to be written in blood, or a good imitation. It read:

*The man you want shoots pool every morning in that Olympic Billiard Parlor across from the freight depot.*

# Chapter 15

Longarm had no idea when or how he'd gotten back to his hotel. He caught a spell of well-earned but restive sleep, and then a six-mule fire engine went clanging by outside to wake him up for the day.

Longarm took his own groaning time getting cleaned up and into a fresh shirt and underwear. His mouth tasted like the bottom of a dried-out spitoon, and flies were buzzing around fresh dog shit inside his skull. Like most self-educated men, Longarm read more than he let on. So he knew mountain folks down in South America chewed coca leaves to keep going and going, like a perpetual-motion machine. He hadn't known you could screw so long with so many different gals and barely recall any pleasure. That *rum* the coca leaves were steeped in hadn't helped him think straight either.

The question before the house now was what he was supposed to do about the helpful hint they'd written in blood for him. Ned Buntline had written a yarn in ink for his dime magazine, allowing that the late James Butler Hickok had once challenged John Wesley Hardin to a face-to-face showdown to be held in the middle of the street at high noon.

Aside from the simple fact that neither mean drunk would have been out of bed by high noon, they were mean but not suicidal drunks, and nobody with a lick of sense would ever respond to such an invitation by coming out from cover with another known gunfighter waiting almost anywhere out yonder, with or without a scoped rifle.

So there was no way Longarm was about to sashay through the doorway of the Olympic Billiard Parlor before he knew who'd be waiting inside with what. Anyone who could write one voodoo note could write another.

Instead he entered the freight depot indicated in the note from a far side, moseyed through the morning bustle to where he could peer out another way, and saw that, sure enough, there really was an Olympic Billiard Parlor across a busy street crowded with wagons. But whether old Big Thumb Gatewood would be shooting Rotation or maybe a game of Eight Ball at such an hour was anybody's guess. Gatewood wasn't wanted for any federal offenses, and there were mornings Longarm felt too young to die. So seeing that anybody shooting pool inside would likely shoot pool a spell longer, Longarm drifted out the back way and ambled on over to Courthouse Square.

Neither the state nor county courts were in session that morning. But the municipal Magistrate's Court hardly ever got to close. So he strode in, found a seat in the back, and waited for a lull as an old gray judge who didn't bother with a robe made short work of the night's haul by the town law.

Four whores in a row were given thirty-dollar fines and suspended sentences of thirty days apiece. A gentleman of color who'd cut another in a crap game threw himself on the mercy of the court and allowed he'd accept thirty days on a segregated road gang. The judge said, "I don't doubt you would, seeing you've been here before for another cutting. I reckon we'd best remand you to Criminal Court B, two weeks from today, and set your bail at five big ones, you slashing son of a bitch!"

As they led the sporting man back to the holding cells, the bailiff presented a tall skinny cowhand before the bench. His name was Harold Thorp and the charge was indecent exposure. He said his pals called him Slim and that he wanted to plead not guilty.

The judge stared soberly down at the arrest report as he sighed and said, "Well, speaking as another friend, Slim. You'd be well advised to plead guilty and get off with a thirty-dollar fine and time served. Whatever possessed you to take your dick out and wave it at those poor ladies coming out of that notions shop on Main Street?"

Thorp insisted, "I never did. They must have me mixed up with some other Slim. I ain't about to pay no fine for something I never done!"

The judge said, "In that case you're going to have to convince a higher court than this one, and I sure hope you have your own witnesses. According to this arrest report you were identified by both offended ladies, the shopkeeper, and a boy loading barrels in a dray. So your trial date will be the tenth of next month and I'll set your bail at two hundred, seeing you're a friend of mine, Slim."

The cowhand looked befuddled, and bawled he didn't have no two hundred dollars, until a shorter gent in a checked suit, walking with a crablike limp, came forward to take Slim by one arm and say, "Let me do your talking as we settle up with the court clerk, cowboy. I'd be Howard Brinks, with Triple 6, and it's only going to cost you twenty with us posting the balance, see?"

Longarm saw more than that as the crablike runner for the Triple 6 led the taller culprit toward the back. For one of the white men at that *banda* orgy the night before had been built like Brinks and scuttled the same way as Brinks. So it sure was a small world, and the late Caddo Kid had *said* his bail-bonding outfit had some colored help, although not the sort of colored help most white folks meant when they said that. It was no wonder Cahill had been able to scare that wavering informant-porter up in Denver with goofer dust and likely threats of voodoo *wangas*!

Once the white runner who enjoyed voodoo drums had led yet another client into the court clerk's cubbyhole, Longarm rose and drifted over to a uniformed bailiff by the front entrance.

He handed the doubtless underpaid bailiff an unlit smoke and said, "Name's Culpepper. My friends call me Cross. I'm packing wanted papers on a road agent named Gatewood who's been spotted here in Big D."

The bailiff put the smoke away for later, saying, "Bounty hunter, eh? Can't say anyone named Gatewood has passed through these here oaken portals. This is only Magistrate's Court. We don't get any road agents here. The few serious felonies we deal with get passed up the line to the judges and juries of Criminal Courts A and B."

Longarm said, "So I heard. You wouldn't know anything about the recent killing of some young squirt named Tommy, would you?"

The bailiff shook his head, hesitated, and decided, "Hold on. Are you talking about Tom Graham, that mammy man killed in a whorehouse brawl in the colored quarter week before last?"

That didn't work for Big Thumb Gatewood. But Longarm nodded and said, "Sounds about right. What's a mammy man? Is that anything like a squaw man?"

The bailiff grimaced and said, "Same difference. Some trash whites seem to think they'll do better hanging out with Indian or colored gals and their kith and kin. White man living in a tipi as a favor to a better-looking gal than he might manage among his own usually has a little more money and uses way bigger words than his newfound friends. Tom Graham was a goofy-looking kid with a stammer and a way bigger allowance than your average shoeshine boy. So he liked to sleep with pretty colored gals down to the quarter where the Trinidad and White Rock Creek come together. Nobody really cares that much about killings in the quarter. But the way I heard it, the fool kid died in a duel over the favors of a two-dollar whore the two of them could have asked for group rates."

"Was the man who killed him white?" asked Longarm.

The Texan said, "Must have been. The Rangers would have gone after any nigger who killed any white man for any reason. I don't know the name of the man who killed Tom Graham. Reckon it's up to his kin now.''

"The Graham boy had a big family?" asked Longarm.

The bailiff shook his head and said, "Just a big sister, Old maid who works at the public library across the square. Can't see *her* down in the quarter, looking for the man who killed her brother."

Longarm allowed that would be hard to picture, and drifted on. He had the time. So he crossed the open square, with the sun starting to weigh seriously on his shoulders now, and got inside the shady library to see how you went about asking for the librarian whose kid brother had been killed in a colored whorehouse.

As he stepped into the main reading room he saw at a glance he wouldn't have to ask. The severely pretty little mouse-haired gal behind the desk wore reading glasses and a summerweight shantung bodice that didn't do a thing for her unusual build. She'd taken a tub bath since last they'd screwed out at Queen Esther's the night before. But there was no mistaking that perfume or the shy-puppy way she moved, with or without a stitch on.

Not recognizing him with his clothes on and his face hanging out, she demurely asked if there was anything she could do for him.

He didn't think he'd better tell her she already had. He didn't want to have her sobbing about her Tommy, Tommy, Tommy again as she clawed his bare back. So he said, "I'm interested in books on magic, ma'am. I like to do magic tricks at parties. I have the sleight of hand figured out pretty good, but I lack the patter. The hocus-pocus talk that goes with party magic. Might you have any books on Oriental or Gypsy or what do you call that colored magic—mumbo jumbo?"

She looked away, blushing as if he'd caught her with her fingers in her snatch, as she murmured, "I think the word you're after would be voodoo. But it's not magic. It's a religion. I don't know anything about voodoo myself. But from

119

what I've been told by some servants, voodoo is not something to mess with just for fun.''

"I've heard tell *some* white folks mess with it," Longarm replied with as much of a poker face as he could manage. She still didn't act as if she knew he'd come in her twice. So he pressed his luck with: "Why else would white folks mess with voodoo if it wasn't fun? It's some sort of black devil worship, ain't it?''

She shook her mousy head primly and said, "Not at all! There may be some white dabblers in the black arts who mess with voodoo the way they mess with astrology, the Tarot, or the Hebrew Abracadabra. I suppose if you're looking for a shortcut around the hard work of reality, it helps to believe in magic. But too many followers of the occult are as lazy about study as they are about work. Some say—I wouldn't know— that a voodoo *hungan* or *mambo* can produce *real results,* if you approach them with a sincere and open mind, willing to learn.''

"And willing to cross their palms with silver?" Longarm asked.

She pursed her lips and asked, "Do they have a poor box inside the door of the Roman church across the square? Have you ever attended a Protestant service where they didn't pass the collection plate? Of course people attending a voodoo *banda* contribute to the upkeep of the *humfo* and . . .''

She caught herself and said, "Dear me, from the way I go on you'd think I really *cared* about such superstitions.''

Longarm assured her he could see she was an upstanding Christian woman, and left, having learned more the sneaky way than she might have told him if he'd asked right out. Although, headed out into the hot sun with La Siesta coming up, he idly wondered where the sweet little saggy-titted gal meant to spend her own lie-down.

He worked his way back to where he could cover the entrance of the Olympic Billiard Parlor from the shade of the freight depot overhang. A million years went by as the hustle and bustle around him faded and the sun outside kept blazing down harder. Big Thumb Gatewood wouldn't fit as the killer of Tom Graham unless he'd been in Dallas longer than any lawmen had thought. On the other hand, if he'd been well hidden out in Dallas, nobody could have reported seeing him earlier.

Another million years went by as half-a-dozen gents drifted out of the pool hall across the way without answering to Gatewood's description. Then, as suddenly as a late train pulling into the station at last, there he was, with his right hand in his pocket and that Schofield riding low and tied down just below it. Longarm had figured that any man shooting pool in the morning would be headed home for La Siesta by this time.

Just where that might be was as important to the law as the capture of one fugitive from justice. Knowing he could throw down on his target at any time, Longarm resolved to follow him home to his hidey-hole and report *that* to Billy Vail as well.

It wasn't as easy as expected. Gatewood walked one block south to turn a corner and step into a livery stable, while Longarm stepped into the shade of a storefront.

A few minutes later Big Thumb Gatewood led a roan mare with white stockings out of the livery to mount up and ride, neither fast enough to attract attention nor slow enough for a man on foot to follow far.

Longarm let the road agent pass, and then ran for the livery stable himself, hauling out his wallet on the fly. Inside, he cornered a startled Caddo hostler. "Five dollars says you can't saddle me a mount and see me out of here in less'n two minutes!"

He lost the bet, as he hoped he might. The Caddo grunted something about once having worked for the Butterfield Stage Line as he had Longarm on his way before he'd pocketed the five-dollar bet, the ten-dollar deposit, and the two-bit day rate. So it wasn't exactly simple, but suspecting he knew the general direction, Longarm soon had that roan mare in sight, and sure enough, they were all headed south in line with the water courses and railroad tracks toward the flats set aside as one of the big town's several colored quarters.

Knowing where they were likely headed gave Longarm another edge when the man who'd been on the dodge all the way from California was inspired to swing off the road into a clump of cottonwoods, as if he meant to take a leak.

Longarm swung right along a cinder-paved alley to head over to another southbound road as he explained to his hired buckskin, "Old Big Thumb is afraid somebody might be following him. So whilst he's holed up in that vacant lot to watch his back trail, we'll just lope south and get ahead so's he can ride *past* us."

But it didn't work. As they came out the far end of that alley, a round of .45-28 took Longarm's hat off, and he thought it best to just fall after it, off the far side, as yet another slug bounced off his hired saddle swells, spooking his hired horse considerably.

As his livery mount bolted from between them, Longarm propped up on his left elbow with his own gun drawn to stare through the dust at the owlhoot rider who'd outfoxed him. Big Thumb Gatewood was afoot with a six-gun in each fist, but the right one was firing the fastest.

Longarm fired once, then twice, as his first round hit where a calmer gun hand had aimed it. So the overexcited Gatewood, who'd seen a stranger turn off the road and circle to head him off, dropped to both knees as he bawled, "I give! You've hit me where it hurts like fire and you have to *help* me, damn your eyes!"

"Drop them guns! I mean it!" Longarm called back as he rolled up on one knee with his smoking .44-40 trained on the treacherous road agent. Big Thumb Gatewood fired again, aiming wild but too close for comfort, as Longarm muttered "Shit!" and finished him clean with a third shot.

He rose and moved cautiously forward, reloading his wheel as he closed in. Big Thumb Gatewood lay dead at his feet, but he didn't know it yet. For he managed to flutter his eyes, and his last words were: "I knew I couldn't trust them niggers!"

# Chapter 16

La Siesta did not apply when a man lay dead on the streets of Big D. But it proved surprisingly easy to get away with shooting a man under an assumed name, provided the man you shot was wanted dead or alive and you were packing the papers to prove it.

As they were loading the body aboard a morgue wagon, an elderly lady who'd been tending her herb garden across the way came forward on her own to back Longarm's simplified story. She said she'd seen Big Thumb Gatewood tear up the street at a gallop, rein in, and then dismount with a revolver in either fist to cover that alley entrance.

She said Longarm had scared her half to death when she'd thought he was getting blown out of his saddle with a bullet in his brain. One of the two Dallas roundsmen who'd responded to the sounds of gunplay was of the opinion that Gatewood had been rattled by a dead man sitting up to draw his own side arm.

They took statements from Longarm, the old lady, and a Mexican gardener across the way who confessed, when asked, he'd seen the short, noisy confusion about the same way. The copper badges said someone from the Dallas County Coroner, if not the D.A., might come around with more detailed depositions for them to sign. But nobody expected a big fuss over a shit-heel road agent who tried to ambush folks on the streets of Big D.

The pony Longarm had hired was nowhere to be found. He hoped it had run back to its stable stall, as frightened ponies were inclined to. The roan mare Gatewood had been riding was still loosely tethered to a picket fence just down the way. So Longarm elected to ride her back to the stable both critters had come out of before he went on back to his hotel.

As he parted friendly with the town law and his helpful witnesses, Longarm saw the mare he was sitting had been saddled California-style with a center-fire Videlia stock saddle, fitted with saddlebags as well as two now-empty holsters latigoed to the swells on either side of the dally-roping horn.

Back at the livery stable they told him the late Mr. Gatewood had been hiring the roan by the day, but using the saddle he'd brought him from wherever. So Longarm braced it on a hip and carried it back to the Travis Hotel to spend La Siesta with him, after first making them return his deposit on that *other* pony he spotted out back.

When he got up to his room, he saw Red Robin had been smart enough to leave the door ajar once she'd picked the lock in her own casual way. He'd once scared the liver and lights out of her when he'd seen someone was up in his room and hadn't known who it was.

As he sashayed in to drop the outlaw's saddle in a corner but lay the saddlebags across the bed, Red Robin, who'd been lounging there demurely in her bare socks and chemise, asked, "Where in the hell have you been and how many saddles does one rider need? I have to get back to work by four and it's almost two-thirty already!"

Longarm shut the door and bolted it as he tersely told her, "Just caught up with that Big Thumb Gatewood I told you about. He was good. Spotted me tailing him, and then he outrode and came near to winning when I rode into his gunsights like a greenhorn in Apacheria."

Red Robin rolled upright and held out her bare arms to him as she offered to kiss it and make it better. So he shucked his

124

own duds, hoping like hell he could still get it up. For that last Mexican, high yaller, or breed out at that voodoo *banda* had been overdoing it no matter how much Queen Esther wanted them all to sacrifice.

As he undressed, Red Robin pulled her chemise off over her henna-rinsed mop, and being she was built like, well, Red Robin, he was able to rise to the occasion after all.

But as he lay down beside her to take her well-proportioned creamy form in his darker-tanned arms, Red Robin demurely pleaded, "I know I was insatiable last time. But I fear it was that bitchy tension a girl feels just before . . . you know. It's just not fair that we have to suffer so while you brutes go scot-free with your old privates ever ready for action!"

He held her close enough to flatten her milky breasts against his chest, and kissed her gently before he dryly observed, "I know. I was talking to the Lord that morning he put old Adam to sleep and pulled out that rib. I said, Lord, as long as you're fixing to create gals for us old boys to have fun with, wouldn't it be *more* fun if you were to fix 'em so's they'd be moody and out of commission once a month?"

She cuddled closer, but pouted, "It's not funny. It hurts. Even when I don't invite company down there. And Custis, you're so *manly* down there, even when I'm not fixing to have my period."

He suggested, "In that case why don't we just bill and coo like lovebirds from the waist up?"

She stared up at him adoringly and asked, "Would you be willing to settle for less than full gallop, darling? I don't want to let you down. I know how you men have to have it, and maybe if I just went down on you for some practice on the French horn . . ."

He held her tighter and said, "I don't like to start things I can't finish, honey. It wouldn't be fair to you, and even if it was, I'd want it in your swell little ring-dang-doo when I was fixing to come. So why don't we just spoon like kids out together for the first time?"

Red Robin giggled and said, "Stark naked, belly-to-belly,

with that old familiar feeling tucked between my thighs?''

He offered to haul it out from between her thighs if it bothered her. But Red Robin said it felt sweet, and asked him to kiss her some more. So he did, and thanks to that last barely remembered encounter out at Queen Esther's the night before, Red Robin marveled at his amazing self-control as they lay there swapping spit like a couple of kids. That's what women called it when a man managed not to howl at the moon like a coyote, self-control.

As they controlled themselves, Longarm brought Red Robin up to date with more details about his secret work, leaving out the parts that might have shocked her. She agreed they ought to look in the dead man's saddlebags to see if he'd left any important evidence. So they propped themselves up against the head of the bedstead and shared a cheroot as they sorted through the possibles of Big Thumb Gatewood.

For a cuss who cut other riders off when they least expected it, Big Thumb Gatewood hadn't had much imagination. They mostly found fresh socks, a shaving kit, extra boxes of .45-28 Army rounds, and copies of the same reward posters Longarm had been packing as part of his own cover.

When Red Robin asked him about that, he explained, ''Billy Vail don't approve of his deputies putting in for bounty money, seeing we get paid to go after outlaws in any case. On the other hand, a real Crossdraw Culpepper would surely apply for these rewards, and there's no telling who's keeping an eye on the Western Union office over by the depot. So I reckon I'll wire Wells Fargo as Nero Culpepper, and they'll take the usual few weeks before they send a money order I'll never be able to cash.''

He took a thoughtful drag on their shared cheroot and added in a hopeful tone, ''By then I ought to have a better grasp on whatever in hell I'm doing down this way!''

She shrugged a soft naked shoulder against his as she asked what had him so puzzled. She said, ''From what you've told me, some traveling men with prices on their heads tend to rent rooms or live with local hookers in the seamier parts of town.

Here in Dallas that would be the slums where colored folks have congregated. You say Gatewood may have killed another white man over the favors of a colored whore?''

Longarm blew a smoke ring at their bare toes atop the covers as he decided, ''Mebbe. A man who'd call folks niggers with his dying breath would have no business fighting duels over pretty quadroons. Somebody who didn't like him at all tipped me off to where he could be found, knowing, or thinking they knew, I was a bounty hunter. I'd say it was as likely Gatewood just bullied his way into some boardinghouse or whatever in the colored quarter down the bottom a piece without trying to make friends. There's a breed of white man, or woman, who does the darkie the great favor of taking advantage of them with a smile. But I suspicion Gatewood was the kind who just takes what he wants from anyone he has any edge on, whether they like it or not. I suspicion some follower of Queen Esther simply asked her for a *wanga* or curse on a pesky stranger, and she had someone *wanga* him good by tipping me off with a voodoo grigri, or charm. A dry chicken leg makes a powerful charm when you include a note to a known bounty hunter.''

Red Robin said, ''You just told me Gatewood might have been voodoo-cursed for killing someone's kid brother down in the quarter. Have you changed your mind?''

He grimaced and said, ''Never made my mind up. Works either way. I ain't sure it matters, as far as my mission is concerned. Turning a wanted man in to the law ain't against the law, even when you do it spooky. That Caddo Kid told me right off that someone with the Triple 6 was getting hot tips from colored informers. I'm sure I know who their go-between is. I told you I think I spotted their runner, Howard Brinks, at that voodoo *banda* I told you about.''

She frowned thoughtfully and said, ''Tell me *more* about it. Is it true those voodoo darkies worship the Devil by screwing virgins on an altar?''

Longarm was able to truthfully reply, ''I didn't see nothing like that going on. They assured me they didn't believe in our

127

Devil. Some white folks who dabble in voodoo might. I suspicion that anyone upset enough to turn from their own upbringing and chase after a mishmash of anything that don't sound logical, is likely to believe in devil worship, fairies in the bottom of their garden, or perpetual-motion machines. Ain't no organized religion, including voodoo, that allows a lazy-thinking greedy-grubber to get anything for nothing.''

Red Robin asked, in that case, what the number of the beast, or 666, might signify.

He answered simply, ''Don't know. Could be just a number, or somebody could have started out looking for a devil-worshipping temple, then joined a voodoo *humfo* when they failed to find one in these parts. One of those books I told you about points out that Satanism or our notion of devil worship was powerful among Protestants and Papists alike during the late 1600's when the first slaves were being imported to the different colonies on this side of the pond. So such Satanism as you'll find in La Societé Voudou drifted down the back stairs and out to the slave quarters from the master bedroom, where books on Satanism were more likely to be found. Some of those French aristocrats before their revolution were really interested in such notions. The Bluebeard in that French fairy tale is based on a real French nobleman. Like I said, bored and infantile white folks can match any medicine man or witch doctor when it comes to superstition.''

Red Robin asked, ''Are you saying this white outfit that uses the Devil's brand as its own may have corrupted a voodoo cult meant for field hands into some national outlaw-tracking service?''

Longam laughed and kissed her cheek as he said, ''That wouldn't be against the law.''

She demanded, ''What *are* they doing that's against the law then? As far as I can see, those bail bondsmen and their colored informers have just been ridding society at large of bail-jumping outlaws!''

He said, ''That's about the size of it. But Judge Dickerson back in Denver ain't the only federal judge who wants to know why. Nobody hunts outlaws or even wild geese at a considerable loss. They sent me down here in hopes I could join the outfit and find out what's really going on. My nailing that wanted road agent was just icing on the cake, and I may as well confess, I can't seem to *get* at the blamed cake!''

They kissed and cuddled some more, and might have gone all the way if they hadn't noticed how late it was getting before they could really get going. She said he was a real gent when he just helped her dress and carried her back to her own hotel around four.

He was on his way to the Western Union office, aiming to wire Billy Vail a progress report, when he heard his fake name called out in an angry tone.

He turned to see the lean and mean Lash Legrange standing shorter than natural with his gun hand half raised to the grips of that big .50-50 Griswald in the shoulder rig half hidden by his black-leather bolero jacket.

Legrange jeered, ''I heard you got your man down by the quarter, Crossdraw. You still say you're Crossdraw Culpepper, don't you?''

Longarm soberly answered, ''My friends call me Cross. If you don't want to be my friend, I suggest you keep your fucking hand away from that fucking cannon. If you have a beef with this child, spit it out like a man. Don't try for drawing-room-comedy sarcasm. You ain't got the brains for it and I don't have the patience.''

Another voice cut in. ''Fow Gawd's sake, Lash, I told you to run on ahead and stop him, not start a war with him!''

The older and softer Sam Wedford joined them, puffing some, and added, ''What's eating you, Lash? You know how many cases we have and you know how shorthanded we are right now!''

Legrange insisted, ''He ain't no friend of the Caddo Kid. I rode high and I rode low with the Caddo Kid, and he never made no mention of no bounty hunter called Crossdraw Culpepper. The only Crossdraw Culpepper I've been able to find shit about is doing time in a Colorado state prison!''

Longarm quietly muttered, "I could show my release papers, but it's more fun to tell you to go fuck yourself. You're just so lovely when you're angry, sweetheart."

Sam Wedford sighed and said, "That's enough from the both of you. I told you Howard checked him out with Queen Esther, Lash."

Then he turned to Longarm. "We offer a hundred dollars a month base pay. That's more than twice a top hand's wages and twenty-five more than your average lawman can hope to draw. After that we pay all travel expenses and a hundred-dollar bonus on each and every bail-jumper you bring back."

"Dead or alive?" asked Longarm, thoughtfully.

Sam Wedford shrugged and said, "That's up to them, I reckon. We pay the same whether they come quiet or not. How do you like it so far?"

Longarm said, "Well, I don't know how long Wells Fargo is likely to be with some real money I earned this morning."

Lash Legrange warned, "He's fencing with words. I told you he's up to something. I can smell a lawman the way the Giant smelled Jack, and you know what happened to that Giant, Boss!"

Sam Wedford said, "Calm down. I told you Queen Esther vouches for him not riding for any law we have to worry about. She tested him last night, knowing no state or federal lawman would ever fuck a suspect."

Lash marveled, "Queen Esther let this total stranger fuck her?"

Wedford smiled dirty at Longarm and replied, "She did, and she says she sort of enjoyed it too."

# Chapter 17

Longarm allowed he'd sleep on the offer, and thanks to Red Robin's indisposition, he got to sleep alone as he pondered which of those wild woman out at the voodoo *banda* might have been Queen Esther. He was sure she'd taken off that crazy outfit before she'd joined him on the main floor—literally.

That nicely built and skillfully screwing white gal wearing that inverted star had an alibi. So did the floppy-titted librarian he'd had next, and he was almost sure that wild skull mask under a stovepipe hat had been grinning down at them from the stairs while he was dog-styling that plumper gal with a Mexican accent but a darker rump than your average *mestiza*.

He reflected that it was easy to put on an accent as well as a mask, but thinking back, that one had had no call to. Queen Esther had been watching him and likely sizing him up for herself when he'd wound up with that really fat white gal who'd insisted on calling him her *Damballa Loa* and pretended she was talking some African lingo. When folks faked a lingo, they said the same words over and over, like a baby going goo-goo. At least one of those *hungans* had been chanting something that sounded like real talk from his old country, and hadn't that been about the time Longarm had wound up on his back with his junoesque gal on top, as warm and brown as buttered toast, as she did all of the work, squatting on those strong shapely thighs?

He decided that could have been her, or it could have been somebody else, once he'd lost count and likely passed out completely. He couldn't remember getting dressed, riding back to town, or flopping across this very bed with a chicken claw in his hand like a fool lollipop. But that had to mean Queen Esther had liked him, at least well enough not to steal his wallet.

He knew they'd been through his wallet, and likely his saddlebags over the foot of the bed. A man had to plan ahead when he was working in secret. So all the papers they'd read making him out to be Nero or Crossdraw Culpepper had doubtless been noted and added to his job references by the spooky silent partner of the Triple 6 Bonding and Finance Company.

He thought about that as he reported for work with the outfit the next morning. As he'd wired Billy Vail in code the night before, any professional gunslick who'd turn down such generous terms might not add up as a professional gunslick. An elected county sheriff was lucky to draw more than three or four hundred a month, and he could hire all the experienced deputies he wanted for fifty to seventy-five. Private agencies and cattlemen's protective societies paid up to a hundred a month during an all-out war. Uncle John Chisum had cheated those hired ''Regulators'' recruited by his pal McSween during the Lincoln County War, once the Murphy-Dolan faction started winning. So a hundred-a-month base pay with a bonus for tenser moments was better than Uncle Sam or the Texas Rangers offered a gent who wasn't afraid of noise.

He showed up earlier than he usually got to the Federal Building in Denver, and Sam Wedford told the copper-haired Felicidad to put him on their payroll and issue him some company identification to show any pesky local lawmen who might ask why he was throwing down on a bail-jumper.

One of the secrets of not getting caught at being nosy was not to ask nosy questions that tended to answer themselves.

So he didn't ask where Lash Legrange might be or what they wanted *him* to do next.

Felicidad volunteered that their head recovery rider was west of the Trinity making sure a blacksmith with a drinking problem was at his forge that morning. She explained that most of the bail agreements required a defendant awaiting trial to stay within the county limits while he or she roamed free on bail. She added that she didn't expect Lash back for a few hours. So Longarm allowed he'd drift over to the courthouse and get a better handle on the way their business worked.

Sitting in a back row at Magistrate's Court had baking in the sun on a park bench or hanging around the office with old Sam locked up in the back and Felicidad playing her typewriter beat. But even so, the court docket was sort of tedious, with even a stranger sitting in the back sure he'd seen some of the poor bedraggled whores and busted-up drunks a good many times before. Longarm spied the gnomish runner, Howard Brinks, jawing with a Mexican in a gloomy black suit near the front. The Mexican looked more like a lawyer than a prisoner before the bar, and sure enough, the bailiffs brought in a smirking Mexican kid in a *vaquero* outfit smeared with horse shit and missing some conchos. The charge was disturbing the peace over in the stockyards, and bail was set at five hundred. It appeared the kid disturbed the peace every chance he got and His Honor was getting tired of the sassy squirt.

As the kid, his lawyer, and the runner were settling up with the court clerk, Lash Legrange caught up with Longarm and hissed, "What are you doing here? You're not supposed to hang around this fucking courthouse! That's what we pay Howard to do for us!"

Longarm rose calmly and replied, "Nobody gave me any better chores this morning. What are you afraid I'll catch old Howard at, bribing the judge or blowing goofer dust on a witness?"

Lash Legrange handed him an envelope with a list of names and local addresses penciled on it. He said, "You ain't getting paid to jack off in any back rows. We want to make sure the clients listed here are at work where they claim they have jobs that support them. It sure beats all how men will lie just to get out of jail in the morning.''

Longarm pocketed the list, asking, ''What am I supposed to do if I catch someone playing hooky? Track him to the ends of the earth and shoot him down like a dog?''

Legrange said, ''Don't try to be funny. I don't find anything about you amusing. You report anybody who ain't where he's supposed to be to me. I'll take over from there.''

Longarm started to ask a question, but held his tongue. Nobody out to shoot a man for a minor infraction of a bail-bonding agreement was likely to brag about it in advance. It seemed easier to just carry out the simple orders. So he got cracking.

The morning was nigh shot. But a couple of the clients had given their places of employment as within easy walking distance. So Longarm checked them out on foot, found they were both behaving fairly well for gents charged with wrecking a bar and punching a landlady, and went over to the library to talk that mousy gal with floppy tits into issuing him a library card and allowing him to carry some reading material back to his hotel for La Siesta.

He asked to see some more of those bragging pioneer books, knowing second-generation members of the more imposing pioneer families tended to write privately printed and expensively bound books to present to all the local schools and libraries with shelf space to spare. Longarm had often wondered if anybody who wasn't connected with the authors of such boastful books read all that many. But he'd found them a good source of information as he'd roamed west of the Big Muddy.

But he found nothing of public or private record to connect the well-known and far-flung Wedford clan of Texas with voodoo or even the Holy Rollers of the Pentecostal Movement.

But Queen Esther had as much as admitted that that run-down plantation she claimed as her own private property had been sold or leased to her by some Wedfords, and Sam Wedford's runner at the courthouse, the crablike Howard Brinks, was an active member of her voodoo cult.

Longarm read up on less sinister local history, caught a few winks, and got back to work late that afternoon aboard his borrowed saddle and another pony hired off young Calvin out back. The hotel livery hired its riding stock to hotel guests without a deposit and at reasonable rates. Calvin said he'd hire the Cap'n a horse and buggy with driver for five dollars a night if he wanted to drive off across White Rock Creek again in style.

Longarm asked when they might be holding another *banda* out yonder. Calvin repeated that he was a born-again Baptist. But allowed he'd let him know if he heard anything. Calvin seemed to have no idea who'd put that black pony in its stall with fodder and water the last time.

Longarm rode back to the center of town with the list Lash Legrange had given him as the town came back to life that afternoon. Dallas was spread out considerably when it came to private mailing addresses. But its downtown business district, concentrated near where its east-west Main Street met the north-south Trinity, was smaller than the business district of Denver.

The two towns were laid out differently and he had to ask his way around some to locate bailed-out punchers working in the stock yards, bad-tempered swampers working in saloons a good ways off, and so on. But he was able to complete the list before the late Texas supper time, and had to wonder, as he did so, why in thunder Sam Wedford paid so well for chores young Henry back in Denver or, hell, Felicidad here in Dallas could carry out as well.

The next day went much the same, and the day after that, with the only suspicious, or interesting, development being the time he passed that mousy-haired gal from the library on the stairs as he was leaving the office for another tedious ride around town. Since he'd not only been borrowing books from her, but recalled her sobbing about her Tommy as he'd been screwing her to voodoo drums, Longarm was naturally tempted to pussyfoot back up the stairs and see if he could hear what she'd come for. She seemed upset. She hadn't appeared to recognize him on the dimly lit stairs. He kept going down them. The way you kept a suspect from noticing you watching them was not to watch them too close. It was safer to hope she'd leave something in writing up yonder.

He'd found himself in the office alone more than once. He hadn't poked his nose in any file drawers as yet. But old Sam and the copper-haired Felicidad had started to act as if he belonged there, like the Currier and Ives prints on the wall or that brass spittoon nobody used, near Felicidad's desk.

But he wasn't ready to make such a move just yet. Lash Legrange still seemed to resent him, and Felicidad had gone silent and awkward on him since he'd felt her up and she'd asked him what he thought her boss was really up to. Lash was likely the only one there who let his true feelings show. Longarm had to know whether Wedford had put her up to it before he risked her catching him in her drawers—desk drawers or underdrawers.

A surly barkeep who tended to sample what he was serving and beat his common-law wife wasn't at the saloon he'd given as his place of employment. His trial was set for the next day. But they told Longarm he'd sent word he was home sick. So Longarm rode over to the cottage he shared with the gal, to find him in bed with the gal, who'd elected to drop all charges. Longarm had no instructions covering such a dumb situation. So he wished them well and rode back to the office.

When he got there the boss told him he'd done right, and said he was to wait around. Wedford added, ''We just got a tip on a possible jump. Legrange is looking into it right now. He says you were in court when we went the bail of Sonny Galvez the other day?''

Longarm thought, nodded cautiously, and asked, ''Mex *vaquero* who got into a stockyard brawl the other night?''

Wedford said, ''That's our Sonny. He rides for good neighbors of mine and every time we bail him out the bail goes up. Someone we keep in tobacco money at the depot says our

Sonny has gone home to his kin on the Brazos. Across the county line and fare-thee-well to the bail we posted on the ingrate if the court finds out about it before we can convince him of the error of his ways!"

Sam Wedford left Longarm out front with Felicidad to something more private in his own cubbyhole. Longarm sat down. Felicidad asked him where he'd met Flora Graham.

He asked who they might be talking about. When she described a mousy-haired gal he'd met on the stairs, he brightened and said, "I thought I'd seen her over to the library. I didn't know her name."

Felicidad said, "She recognized you. She seemed taken with you and surprised you rode for us. As a recovery rider, I mean. She wasn't here to arrange bail for anyone."

Longarm didn't ask what Tom Graham's spinster sister had been there for. So naturally the gal who worked there said, "She's applied to us for a loan. We're a finance company as well as a bonding company, you see."

Longarm didn't see if he was supposed to see what she was getting at. When he just sat there, Felicidad asked, "Would you loan her ten thousand dollars if it was up to you?"

Longarm laughed lightly and replied, "Not hardly. I ain't got that sort of money to lend anyone if it *was* up to me! Is that who Sam's jawing with up front?"

Felicidad shook her copper-haired head and replied, "She's long gone, with a check. Sam approved her loan. I don't know why. She's not very pretty, and the vacant lots she put up as security are barely worth that much tax free. So many of them come in for loans after the banks turn them down, with good reason. You know about back tax liens, clouded title searches, and so on, of course?"

Longarm shook his head with a laugh and replied, "Lord love you, I told you before I came to work here that I'm better with a gun than with a pencil, Miss Felicidad."

She stared darkly down at her desk and muttered, "I'm good with a pencil. I'm paid to be good with a pencil, and when figures don't add up and nobody seems to care, I have to wonder why!"

He didn't tell her how much she sounded like more than one federal lawman he knew, including himself. He said something about just working there. Then Lash Legrange came in, scowling, to say, "Well, here's where you get to earn your salt, Cross."

Lash held out a sheaf of papers. Longarm recognized the standard bail-bonding form and the contract Triple 6 required. There was a sheet of yellow foolscap as well. When Longarm took them, he saw that the surly Legrange had blocked-lettered in directions to the Galvez home spread near the falls of the Brazos, south of Waco. Longarm didn't say he knew the Waco area. Every time you told Lash Legrange you knew something or somebody, he wanted to know how come.

Folding the papers and putting them away, Longarm asked about train tickets.

Lash Legrange snorted, "What do you think this is, a U.S. marshal's office? You get there as best you can. You bring the rascal back, dead or alive. Then and only then you ask the boss for your bonus and any additional expenses. Are there any other questions?"

Longarm said, "Yep. If Sonny Galvez has skipped on a five-hundred-dollar bail bond and I bring him back dead . . ."

"We recover our money in full," Legrange finished.

Felicidad demurely explained, "When a defendant fails to appear in court, he forfeits his bail. When a defendant can't stand trial because he's deceased, we get the money *back,* see?"

"I'm beginning to," Longarm said soberly. Then, as Cross-draw Culpepper of the Triple 6 Bonding and Finance Company, he strode forth to see if he could get their money back for them.

# Chapter 18

Getting there was the hardest part. Thanks to the patchwork public transportation of post–Reconstruction Texas, it took Longarm the better part of forty-eight hours to cover what would have been a little more than a hundred miles as the crow might fly. Since he couldn't buy a ticket to board a crow, Longarm had plenty of time to go over both the terms of the fool kid's bail terms and the report filed by Howard Brinks, who seemed their contact with that far-flug network of railroad porters, baggage handlers, and such that Queen Esther, in turn, had ties to.

Going over the railroad station gossip, Longarm saw that the wayward Sonny Galvez, called Sonny after his father Hector Galvez, a well-known Mexican trail boss, had said he had to get home to a kid sister's Papist confirmation in the town of Brazos Falls. Longarm knew Papists set great store by such family gatherings. He knew there'd be more folks named Galvez, along with kith and kin out to kissing cousins, to threaten a mighty confused and noisy discussion if a strange Anglo just barged in to lay heavy hands on a hot-tempered youth attending a family religious gathering.

But Longarm wasn't called El Brazo Largo by admiring Mexican rebels because he barged in without trying to savvy the ways of a proud but sometimes peculiar people. So once

he got to Waco by rail, he hopped a coach down to Brazos
Falls and registered in the one hotel in town as Cross Culpepper. Then he got tidied up, had something to eat, and went on
over to the only Spanish Catholic church in town, named for
Fourteen Holy Martyrs, presided over by a Padre Hernan
O'Brian, who turned out to be a friendly old cuss who spoke
English, and likely Spanish, with a brogue. When Longarm,
as Crossdraw Culpepper, explained he was in town on a delicate matter about a member of his flock, Padre O'Brian led
him into the rectory and sat him down with a tall glass of iced
rum punch before he took his own seat and asked his guest to
start at the beginning.

Longarm began with Sonny Galvez in Magistrate's Court,
and spelled out the terms of his bail. Padre O'Brian nodded
soberly and said, ''I can see why they sent you. The boy
should not have left the county without permission of the
court. But he is a simple soul who does not read English, and
I feel sure he meant no harm in attending his little sister's
confirmation party last night.''

Longarm nodded and said, ''That's why I thought I'd come
to you with the problem, Padre. I wouldn't want any simple
souls mistaking my true motives if I was to ride out to the
Galvez homestead waving contracts they might not understand.''

The priest asked if Longarm had any less confusing ap-
proaches to offer. Longarm explained he'd be at the hotel
overnight, and suggested Sonny Galvez might prefer to just
ride back to Dallas with him, and they'd say no more about
it once they got there if the court clerk hadn't noticed he was
gone.

So they shook on it, and that evening as the sunset stage
was fixing to arrive, Padre O'Brian turned up at Longarm's
hotel with a sheepish Sonny Galvez, who allowed he'd meant
no harm. So that was about all there was to it. The two of
them rode back to Dallas together, jawing a lot about things
Longarm hadn't heard concerning the social situation in the
upper Trinity Valley. Sonny Galvez seemed a dumb but decent

enough young cuss when he was sober, and Longarm kept him from getting drunk on the way back.

Galvez didn't seem to know anything about that voodoo cult across White Rock Creek. He rode for the Box Double 8, west of the Trinity where the range was more suited to cows. When Longarm asked if he or his Mexican pals knew anything about the Hispanic version of voodoo, Santeria, he said he'd heard some Cubans and Lowland Mexicans from the Vera Cruz coastal swamps fooled around with Santeria. He sounded sort of indignant when he declared no real *Mexican* believed in Santos Negros. It wouldn't have been polite or profitable to ask if his Mexican kith and kin bought into Old Man Coyote or Hummingbird Wizard. He'd been told by other Mexicans from the highlands to the south that only a few pure Indian *peones* went along with their Yaqui and Chihuahua cousins as far as the old Aztec spirits were concerned.

Once Longarm had Sonny Galvez back in the bunkhouse at the Box Double 8, he reported in to Sam Wedford, half expecting to be reprimanded or fired. But the bail bondsman said he'd done right, and told Felicidad to write him up for a bonus.

Later, back at the Travis Hotel, he went over the whole tedious adventure with Red Robin, dog-style, since she'd recovered from her indisposition in time to welcome him back to Big D with open thighs.

Red Robin said she was glad Billy Vail had sent him on a wild-goose chase. But she insisted as she had all along that she didn't see how he'd ever hang a federal offense on anybody. She said the talk around the Red Mill where she worked had Lash Legrange down as a hard-ass hairpin nobody wanted to fight with, but not as an out-and-out crook. His boss, Sam Wedford, was known as a hard-ass horse trader in business. The boys around her piano at the Red Mill seemed to agree you didn't want to borrow money or ask old Sam to go your bail if you didn't meant to pay up, but again, nobody could point to anything really dirty he'd ever done.

Longarm finished in her right with a pillow under her writhing rump, and got a cheroot going for the two of them before

141

he cautiously asked her if she'd heard any more about that voodoo cult he'd made mention of.

Red Robin snuggled closer to fondle his sated shaft as she dismissed such talk as the ravings of bored housewives and their uppity household help. She said, "Nobody who's ever made a dime from the sweat of their brow believes any cotton-chopping slaves could have had magic powers. Nobody who's done a mite better with a little skill or talent they've *worked* at developing believes there's a shortcut to fame and fortune by way of some card-reading or drum-banging hag in a ragged dress. If you had magic powers, if you could even guess the winner of a coin toss better than half the time, would you be set up in a storefront or a shack in the woods telling fortunes for *other* folks?"

He chuckled, patted her bare shoulder, and decided, "Lots of suckers still buy books on how to get rich, never doubting that a man who knew how to get rich would have to write books for a living. But you're right that dabbling in occult notions ain't against any federal statutes, unless you aim to sell one of them bullet-proof medicine shirts to an Indian. I suspicion Wedford's courtroom runner, Brinks, got that tip on Sonny Galvez being off the reservation from some of his voodoo pals. I suspect he carried on with voodoo *gals* even worse. But there was no real harm done in the eyes of federal law. Galvez had agreed not to leave the county before his trial. Thanks to that tip I managed to get him back here before his bail was forfeited. Thanks to a kindly old priest I managed to get him back without even scaring his little sister. So what the late Caddo Kid said about some bail-jumpers coming quieter than others seems to apply."

Red Robin said, "The extra time I talked the Red Mill into is up. I have another job lined up in Fort Collins. If you were to leave with me, I might manage a layover in Denver and really satisfy myself with you for once."

He kissed the part of her henna-rinsed hair and said soothingly, "One of the reasons we screw so swell every time we meet is that we've never got quite enough of one another. I've noticed, and I'm sure you have too, that the pleasure really does last about as long as that honeymoon of song and poetry. What's the longest we've ever managed to keep going like this, those three weeks in Cheyenne?"

She tweaked his limp manhood and said, "Stay with me in the Denver Palace and I'll keep this inspired until I'm damned well ready to move on. You're wasting your time here, Custis! There's nothing going on here that's not going on all over this unfair world. Those Wedfords are the big frogs in this particular puddle, with old Sam Wedford a greedy one who eats smaller frogs dumb enough to get in any sort of debt to him. Are you going to arrest Silver Dollar Tabor up in Leadville because he grubstakes smaller mine owners and winds up with their mines when they can't pay him back on time?"

Longarm grimaced and muttered, "If only. But you're right about it being an unfair world, and I doubt it would run any better if that Karl Marx over in London Town had his own way."

She said, "Come away with me and forget all this money-grubbing and voodoo drumming, Custis. Your real boss suspected there was more to Wedford's bail bonding and moneylending than met the eye. You've been working for the greedy thing over a week. You've worked as one of his recovery riders. You haven't had to gun any bail-jumpers because none of the penny-ante offenders you've dealt with wanted to fight with you. If you ride for Wedford long enough, you'll no doubt wind up *having* to shoot somebody, and what will that prove? You know high altitude is inclined to make a woman passionate, and Denver is a mile above sea level."

It wouldn't have been polite to remind her of that night they'd spent in a tent up in the Front Range. Old Red Robin seemed as hot no matter what the fool altitude under her bounding butts, bless 'em both.

Once La Siesta was over and they both had to get back to work, he carried Red Robin back to her own hotel and headed for the office to see what they wanted him to do next. Striding up the block, he spotted that library gal, Flora Graham, having a sit-down soda in an ice cream parlor with old Felicidad from upstairs. So he wasn't surprised to find the front office empty when he reported in.

He heard their boss, Sam Wedford, jawing with somebody in his own office. The door was barely ajar. So Longarm drifted that way in case they might want him for anything.

He heard Sam Wedford saying, "Lash won't be back this afternoon. So leave the papers with Felicidad and she'll see he gets them in the morning. You've done good and I'll make it up to you once we seal the contract, Howard."

Longarm eased back as the crablike Howard Brinks scuttled out of office, grinned at him like a guilty gnome, and asked where Felicidad might be.

Longarm said, "Just saw her in the ice cream parlor down the way. Is Sam free?"

The runner allowed he supposed so. Longarm knocked on the half-open door and stepped inside, to find Sam Wedford staring pensively out the window. Longarm said, "I checked out that dentist accused of fondling a patient, Boss. He's been at work all morning, whether he's really fondling ladies who take laughing gas or not. Who am I after now?"

Wedford shrugged and said, "Nobody. When Lash gets in I'm sending him after a skip we never should have bailed out. Total asshole booked on indecent exposure. I just told Howard you never bail out a dick-waver, for Gawd's sake!"

Longarm nodded absently, brightened, and asked, "Might we be talking about a tall skinny cowhand called Thorp? Slim Thorp?"

The beefy Sam Wedford blinked in surprise and asked, "You *know* the silly pervert, Cross?"

Longarm said, "Only on sight. I was over to Magistrate's Court last week when they hauled him in for indecent exposure. The judge set his bail at two hundred with his trial set after the first of the month."

Sam Wedford nodded grimly and said, "That would be the bail-jumping bastard in the flesh. I'm sending Lash to bring him in come morning."

Longarm asked mildly, "How come? It ain't the first of the month yet."

Wedford growled, "You let me be the judge of that. When a man's due to stand trial in Dallas and he's dealing faro in Childress, one tends to doubt his sincerity. As you just explained to Sonny Galvez, they are not supposed to leave Dallas County, and Slim Thorp can't say he doesn't know how to read English."

Longarm said, "I got the feeling in court he was a tad irresponsible. The point is that I know the galoot on sight, and there's almost direct rail connections from here to that old trail town on the Red River!"

Sam Wedford insisted, "I just told you, I'm sending Lash to bring Thorp back. If I wanted you to go after him I'd *tell* you to go after him. Do you have any trouble with that, Cross?"

Longarm shrugged and said, "You're the boss. Who do you want me to go after this afternoon if you don't want me to go after Slim Thorp?"

Sam Wedford said, "Ask Felicidad if she has any names she wants you to scout before quitting time."

Longarm said he'd wait for the copper-haired gal out front, and left to do so. He hadn't waited long when, as he expected, Felicidad came up the stairs, nodded at him, and went on in to talk to their boss.

That left Longarm waiting awkwardly alone by her desk. So as long as he wasn't doing anything, he got out his notebook and a pencil stub to write down the address of that card house in Childress where the bail-jumping Slim Thorp was said to be dealing faro these days.

If he caught the next westbound to Fort Worth and changed to the spur line they were building to meet the Santa Fe, he could make it up there long before Lash Legrange reported in for work in the morning.

# Chapter 19

He barely had time to stop by the dance hall and let Red Robin in on where he was headed. He was sorry he had when the passionate piano player snapped, ''You damned fool! If you don't want the job, why don't you just quit? Why go after a bail-jumping pervert who's only going to get you fired if he doesn't wave his dick or a gun in your face?''

Longarm said he didn't mean to make the recovery himself. He told her, ''Thorp doesn't know me. Lash won't be expecting me to beat him up to Childress. That gives me a ringside seat at one of the track-downs the Triple 6 riders are so famous for, see?''

Red Robin shook her henna-rinsed head and said, ''I don't see, and don't expect me to be waiting here like a moon calf in heat when and if you get back from . . . Childress?''

He said, ''Head of the westbound rails where the Red River cuts across the Panhandle. Cow town and county seat. Slim Thorp looks cow. I can't picture him seated, dealing faro. But we live and learn.''

She said she'd learned not to wait around for men who ran off on fool's errands, and being it was a public place, they parted without swapping spit. She'd be there when he got back, or he'd meet her some other time and place. That was likely why they got along so well when and wherever they met up in their travels.

He'd paid for his room at the Travis Hotel by the week. So he had no call to tell them he'd be gone overnight or maybe longer. He left his borrowed stock saddle and baggage where it was, and hopped a westbound traveling light.

He dropped off in the Fort Worth yards within the hour, and bet a dispatcher they wouldn't let him ride with a brake crew of a night train bound for the Panhandle with a string of empty cattle cars.

He lost, of course, and the rear platform of a freight caboose was as comfortable a place to ride and smoke by moonlight as Mr. George Pullman provided in his club cars.

If Queen Esther had any Pullman porters keeping an eye on this particular night train, you couldn't tell. Longarm had yet to meet an Irish railroad brakeman who dabbled in voodoo on the side.

The settlement of Childress was around two hundred miles northwest of Fort Worth, and so they got in around sunrise, and Longarm registered in the one hotel across from the open passenger platform under yet another assumed name. It served Reporter Crawford of the *Denver Post* right for writing all that Wild West crap about Denver's answer to Wild Bill, as Reporter Crawford kept putting it. The room clerk handed Mr. Crawford of Fort Worth his key, and said he hoped he'd have a pleasant stay in Childress.

Longarm smiled dubiously and replied, "I sure hope so. No offense, but you don't seem to have no opera house, and Lord knows how long I'm going to have to wait for the stockmen I'm here to buy some beef from. I don't suppose you have much in the way of whorehouses, card houses, and such?"

The hotel clerk looked flustered and said, "Our town council won't allow no fancy women to operate openly. You might try the One-Eyed Jack Casino up the street if you're content with *cards* for pleasure. They don't open until noon, though. We don't hold with that Mex siesta stuff here in the Panhandle. We keep regular hours, like white men ought to, see?"

Longarm said in that case he'd go on up and catch a hot bath and a few winks. So he did, and when he came back downstairs a little after noon, a strange clerk who didn't know him was on duty behind the desk. So Longarm kept the key and passed on by with a friendly smile.

He found the One-Eyed Jack Casino with no trouble. It seemed to be the only card house within walking distance. He went in, ordered a scuttle of beer at the bar, and moved down to the far end to nurse the beer quietly with his back to the wall and no direct light shining under the brim of his pancaked Stetson as he eyed the earlier arrivals.

Nobody there looked like the tall, thin Harold Thorp he'd seen in the Dallas courthouse. The cuss dealing faro in another corner was tall and thin, but older and brighter-looking, dressed less cow and more tinhorn. It was hard to tell how a man might be armed when he was seated at a table dealing cards from a boxlike faro shoe. But Longarm didn't see how it mattered, and none of the others playing faro seemed out for trouble either.

And so it went, for as long as it took Longarm to sip most of the draft beer and get good and hungry as the afternoon wore on. So he was about to ask the barkeep if they could rustle him up some fried potatoes to eat off the end of the bar, when in through the bat-wings like the bearer of glad tidings strode Lash Legrange, grinning like a Cheshire cat with his *charro* bolero thrown open to expose the grips of that swamping Griswald .50-50.

Nobody there paid him much mind as he approached the faro layout. It was a free country and any number could bet their own money against the house whenever they had a mind to. Longarm assumed that, like himself, Legrange meant to blend into the crowd and wait for Slim Thorp to show up. Since Thorp was said to deal faro there, he'd probably be by sooner or later to relieve the older gent dealing at the moment.

So Longarm was as surprised as anyone when Lash Legrange suddenly called out, "Which one of you might be Slim Thorp?"

149

The more dapperly dressed man who'd been dealing looked up with a puzzled smile and replied, "Some call me that. Do I know you, friend?"

Lash Legrange calmly drew his big Griswald .50-50 as he loudly declared, "You ought to! You bail-jumping son of a bitch!"

And then the big six-gun in his hand went off as the faro dealer was rising with a surprised expression. The look of surprise was replaced by a goggled-eyed silent scream as the 400-grain slug punched him over the heart to blow blood and bone fragments out the back of him while everyone else at the table crawfished from a thick billowing cloud of brimstone-scented gun smoke.

"It's all right! I'm packing papers on the bastard!" Legrange called out as the man he'd shot sprawled backwards on the sawdust on the card-house floor.

Longarm quietly drew his own more modest .44-40 before he stepped clear of the bar to calmly but firmly call out, "You're a liar and I am the law. So drop that gun and drop it now, Legrange!"

Lash Legrange swung the smoking muzzle of his swamping Griswald to fire again as Longarm crabbed to one side and fired at the same time. The Griswald's heavier slug tore a long sliver from the bar by Longarm's elbow. Longarm's round hit Lash Legrange low but dead center to fold him over, as Longarm fired a second time and nailed him smack through the crown of his big sombrero.

Lash Legrange fell in a crumpled heap between Longarm and the faro dealer shot in cold blood. Longarm made no move to check the pulse of either man. Nobody had ever looked deader as they oozed blood and crud into the sawdust of the suddenly silent card house.

Longarm had reloaded and pinned his federal badge on by the time a county deputy charged in, waving a Remington .36 as he bawled out, "What's going on? Somebody says they just gunned Slim Thorp!"

Longarm called out, "The one in the black leather would

150

be a cold-blooded killer who should have done as he was told when I told him to pack it in. The man he just executed for reasons of his own seems to be the victim of mistaken identity. I know Slim Thorp on sight. That ain't Slim Thorp lying yonder.''

The barkeep to Longarm's left called out, "You're wrong, mister. I know you done right as far as that killer in black leather went. But that was Slim Thorp he just killed.''

There came a rumble of agreement as Longarm thought back, hard, and tried in vain to make the now-blank features of the executed faro dealer fit the sort of goofy Slim Thorp accused of indecent exposure that other day in Dallas.

He decided aloud, "I'm missing something, sure as all hell! That can't be the Slim Thorp I was expecting to find up here in Childress. Yet it must have been the Slim Thorp this *other* dead cuss expected to find here. We all saw him *shoot* the poor cuss just now!''

The county deputy cautiously asked, "Are you saying this dead cuss may have had the right to throw down on old Slim, meaning you could have . . . made a mistake?''

Longarm shook his head and replied in a firmer tone, "There was no mistake about Legrange gunning . . . whoever he just gunned with premeditated spite. Whoever the real Slim Thorp might have been, he was wanted for no more than violating the terms set by Magistrate's Court in Dallas on a minor charge. Had Legrange wanted to take him at gunpoint he could have just *said* so. He had the drop on the poor cuss when he fired at point-blank range.''

Another witness volunteered, "The one in black leather fired at you after you'd just said you was the law!''

Longarm muttered, "Bless your good heart and memory, pard.''

So others there chimed in that whatever had just happened, the late Lash Legrange had certainly been in the wrong. So they held the inquest that evening, and Longarm was free to leave town and take both bodies with him if he wanted to.

He didn't want to. It cost enough to have the two of them

photographed, embalmed, and stored in the county morgue until such time as somebody more interested in either came forward.

He caught a regular night train back to Fort Worth. All the cars were coach, so there were no Pullman porters on board. Longarm didn't care. He knew Queen Esther would read about the shootout in print before anyone could voodoo-drum the news ahead. Telegraph wires got there with such news faster than any train could roll. So long before Longarm's night train rolled in, a Childress stringer for the aptly named *Fort Worth Star-Telegraph* had wired the story in to be splashed all over the front page with only about half the facts wrong.

The big *Star-Telegraph* served the whole Fort Worth-Dallas area, and so Longarm wasn't surprised to see some Rangers he knew waiting for him on the station platform, along with the copper-haired Felicidad from the Triple 6 office. Her hair shone almost red in the morning sun, and she was wearing a mighty tight bodice of rust-red pongee as she stood there clutching the morning edition and a manila envelope.

Longarm ticked his hat brim to her, and stared through the Rangers as a signal they were savvy enough to read. So they held back as he howdied the pretty typewriter player and asked her what brought her over to Fort Worth.

Felicidad said, "I *told* you Lash Legrange was up to something! Now Mr. Wedford has gone home to his home spread up the Trinity, sick at heart and feeling confused and betrayed. He's left me in charge of the office with orders to give you this check for two weeks pay in lieu of notice."

Longarm pocketed the check as material evidence as he smiled down at her and said, "You all didn't have to fire me, ma'am. I quit as soon as I put my badge on in the One-Eyed Jack Casino. I had to, as a sworn peace officer, when I witnessed a cold-blooded murder."

The Rangers were listening, ears cocked at a distance, as the gal who'd dispatched Lash Legrange to Childress said, "We read as much in the morning extra. You told their reporters that Lash had shot a total stranger as a bail-jumper you both knew to be somebody else?''

Longarm offered her his elbow as he pointed with his chin, saying, ''We're going to miss our connection back to Dallas if we don't move it on down, ma'am. I never told any reporter nothing. I had to explain a heap to Childress County, and I reckon someone working for them got a few facts murky. I knew for a fact that the Slim Thorp dealing faro over in Childress was not the Slim Thorp the Triple 6 had bailed out on a morals charge. I said Lash *should* have known, and that it hardly mattered whether he had or not, because you ain't supposed to gun anyone at all when he's offering no resistance with the bitty derringer he's packing deep in his vest pocket.''

With the Rangers tagging discreetly along behind them, Longarm led her to the loading platform of the Dallas local and boosted her up the steps as he continued. ''Whatever mistakes Lash might have made about that faro dealer, I told him I was the law before he turned on me. So he knew for certain who I was. I'm still working on who he thought that faro dealer might have been.''

They talked about it some more, all the way back to Dallas aboard the pokey local combination. He showed her a picture of the dead Slim Thorp in the Childress County Morgue. She agreed she'd never seen the cuss before. Then she spoiled it all by confessing she hadn't ever met the younger dick-waver they'd bailed out. She confided she only did the paperwork and hardly ever saw any of their clients at the office.

He asked about folks who borrowed money from them as a finance outfit. She said, ''I'm sure I've spoken to a lot of them. But you'd have to ask Mr. Wedford for details. I only give them application forms and set appointments for them to meet with Mr. Wedford in his private office. He turns down more loan applications than he approves.''

Longarm stared thoughtfully at a chongo-horned cow they were passing as he prodded, ''But you do type up such financial contracts as he does approve, don't you?''

She said, ''Of course. But have you any idea how many

contracts I type up on a given day? Just what is it that you want from me? I'm perfectly willing to help in any way I can. But you have to tell me what you *want,* Cross."

He said, "My real name's Custis. It wasn't my fault. My momma picked it out for me before I could talk. But if you'd like to be on a first-name basis, Miss Felicidad, you might help a heap if you saw fit to go through those office files with me as soon as we get into town."

So she said she would and she did, laughing as she locked the door of the upstairs office after them and confided, "I don't see why we need to change the door sign from Closed to Open, do you?"

He took off his hat as he replied, "Not hardly. You did say your boss ain't coming to work this morning, didn't you?"

She said, "I told you he's out at his home spread, along with Mr. Brinks and some other recovery riders. He seems afraid that Lash was part of some plot against him."

Longarm nodded and began to roll up his sleeves as he smiled thinly and said, "Well, whilst the cat is away the mice get to play. How come you're unbuttoning your bodice, Miss Felicidad?"

The sultry copper-haired gal exposed even more of her exotic dusky-peach hide as she demurely replied, "It's stuffy in here and those old files are awfully dusty. So I thought I'd better set this fresh pongee to one side while I helped you out in just my chemise. You don't mind, do you? You were the one who just pointed out the cat was away and we two little mice have this whole place to just our sweet selves!"

# Chapter 20

He'd been right about her having copper-colored hair all over, and once he'd parted it atop her desk with his old organ-grinder, they really got down to going through the office files, between bouts of slap-and-tickle. During a sweet and sassy interval on the floor with her on top, Felicidad confided she'd been married young to an older man who'd died, doubtless happy, without ever having completed her as a woman. That was what independent career gals called getting to come— feeling completed as a woman.

After that, despite the pleasures offered by the gal who kept the blamed files, Longarm didn't find anything in the files to explain why Lash Legrange or any of the other recovery riders had gunned all those petty offenders out on bail. For that matter, it made little sense for a petty offender to sign such a draconian bail contract and then skip out on a likely modest fine or county sentence. Felicidad said she had no idea either.

As he thoughtfully dog-styled her in Wedford's office, smoking one of Sam Wedford's cigars, Longarm suggested, "Try her this way. We know the Slim Thorp gunned as a bail-jumper in Childress wasn't the same man Howard Grimes bailed out of Magistrate's Court in front of me and everybody. Up in Dodge, the dying Charles Edward Taylor swore he was not the same Charles Edward Taylor who shot up the Red Mill here in Dallas. So what if he was telling the simple truth? What if none of of those men shot as bail-jumpers had ever jumped bail to begin with?''

She arched her spine to take him deeper, with her cheek on the desk blotter as she objected, ''That Sonny Galvez you just brought back from the Brazos was the same one you say you saw bailed out, wasn't he?''

Longarm got a better grip on her shapely hipbones and hauled her lovely rump back to meet him as he replied, ''I never had to *shoot* him neither. *Most* of the petty offenders this outfit has been bailing out have been just what they seemed. Most of the minority who've violated the terms of their bail have been what *they* seemed. Only a small but sinister minority that only a few of your recovery riders have gone after have been killed—or executed, if the scene I witnessed over yonder in Childress was a sample of Legrange's methods. So what if old Sam, old Lash, or old somebody has been sending in ringers for Brinks to bail out?''

She blinked and said, ''Come again?''

He said, ''I'm trying to. Let me move your sweet hips for you. I mean what if some confederate who looked something like a real Slim Thorp, Chuck Taylor, or whatever, deliberately got his fool self picked up for a pretty offense so's an unwitting judge and court clerk could hold *him* on affordable bail for *him* to skip out on?''

She moaned, ''Ooh, faster! You mean some imposter setting up a real person by the same name to be gunned as a bail-jumper? But *why*, Custis? What possible profit could there be in such a monstrous murder plot for anyone? Nobody's collected any bounty on any of those suspicious deaths. We only recovered our bail money, at a loss, part of the time. Why post the money at all if that makes any sense as a motive?''

He agreed it made no sense no matter how you sliced it. Then he added, ''I must be slicing it wrong. I got some riding to do now. So let's try for one more time and—''

She moaned, ''Custis! You can't leave me unfulfilled now that I've found you at last! I was planning on taking you home with me to do it right, in bed with a pitcher of iced sangria!''

He said, ''I'll tell you what. You can wait for me at my hotel. I can send down for that iced Spanish punch if you like. Then I'll just hire a pony out back, run a few errands during La Siesta when nobody will be expecting visitors, and get back to you in time for all the fulfilling you can bear!''

She agreed, they got dressed, and this time he hired a paint gelding from Calvin to ride out in the noonday sun while Felicidad lounged in the darkness upstairs.

As he'd hope, he met nobody at all on the country road past fording White Rock Creek. He circled some to ride into that old cotton spread from an unexpected direction. But nobody seemed to be laying for anybody in the abandoned plantation house.

He saw it wasn't completely abandoned when he spied a chestnut nag with a livery sidesaddle tethered to the back veranda rail. He left his own hired paint in a handy clump of alder near a bend of the rail, and eased up and across the weathered planks, .44-40 in hand.

Inside, where he'd sure swilled a heap of rum and coca with a heap of naked ladies, there was nothing to be seen but dust and cobwebs.

The still, stale air smelled faintly of candle wax, perfume, sweat, and spilled body fluids. But that part seemed to be over for now and the foreseeable future. He found bits and pieces of paper, rags, and food scraps in side rooms on the ground floor. Someone had left a pile of shit in a clothes closet. He heard soft footsteps overhead. So he eased up the dusty staircase, calling ahead, ''This is the law. I'm here on official business. Don't do anything silly and you'll find me ready to listen to reason, hear?''

A soft, shy voice called back, ''There's nobody up here but me! Where has everyone gone?''

As he followed his gun muzzle to the top of the stairs, he spotted a small, pale, familiar figure down the dark hallway. He called out to her, ''Afternoon, Miss Flora. No offense, but you sure look like a voodoo haunt in that pale frock in this light.''

Flora Graham from the public library came cautiously closer as she called out, ''Do I know you, sir?''

He nodded amiably and replied, ''In the Biblical sense, if you want to count that voodoo *banda* we both attended out here the other night. But I'd really be U.S. Deputy Marshal Custis Long, and anything I done with any of you ladies was done in the line of duty with a pure heart!''

She was close enough now for him to see she was blushing beet-red as she covered her saggy tits with her arms and gasped, ''Oh, no! I'm so embarrassed! You never saw me sky-clad, did you?''

He soberly replied, ''If you mean naked to the sky above or naked as a jay, I fear I must have, ma'am. None of us were allowed to keep our duds on, as I recall. Why are you covering yourself so shyly this afternoon, seeing you got that ivory brocade bodice on right now?''

She went on guarding the secret of her saggy tits as she blurted out, ''Don't be horrid! Anything I did that night at the behest of Queen Esther was to earn the *wanga* I sorely needed!''

Longarm nodded soberly and gently replied, ''I heard you'd borrowed ten thousand dollars on some family property, Miss Flora. Is that what Queen Esther was demanding from you, on top of all that sacrificing to her *loas* with your bared Christian flesh?''

The mousy-haired but sort of pretty little gal turned away, sobbing, ''That was to prove my sincerity. Queen Esther won't sell a grigri or cast a *wanga* for any white woman who thinks she's too good for anyone Queen Esther offers her to.''

Longarm grimaced and said, ''She must make a bundle off horny gents who just want to join the party. How much *money* have you given her so far?''

Flora Graham confessed, ''Five thousand in advance and the rest when due. I have her five thousand here, in a money

158

belt I'm wearing under my skirts. But as you see, there's nobody here today!''

Longarm nodded and said, ''I might be able to get your advance payment back. You paid her to curse the man who killed your kid brother, Tom, down the creek in that house of ill repute, right?''

She didn't answer. He gently prodded, ''You told me downstairs as we were screwing, ma'am.''

She sobbed, ''Tom wasn't my younger brother. He was my *son*. We told everyone he was my younger brother once we'd moved here from New Orleans. The neighbors back home had been so cruel about a young girl who trusted married friends of the family.''

Longarm got out the photograph of Slim Thorp, the real Slim Thorp gunned in Childress, as he quietly observed, ''I can see how a lady with no man of her own might resort to magical means for revenge.''

He held out the picture to her, asking if it might be a picture of the man who'd gunned her baby boy.

She gasped, ''Oh, Lord, it is! And he looks so smug and peaceful for a murderer!''

Longarm said, ''He's at peace. He ain't feeling so smug. That's a portrait of his corpse, Miss Flora. He must have felt some discomfort after shooting your Tom down in the quarter. He'd left town to deal faro in other parts. I know you don't care, Miss Flora. But I have asked about, and it does seem your boy, Tom, drew first. They'd have arrested Slim Thorp had he started the fight. But that's just water under the bridge, and I reckon I'd have felt the same if it had been *my* kid. So I thank you for clearing that much up, and I'd better carry you safely back to town now.''

She didn't argue until they got downstairs and he was helping her aboard her sidesaddle. Then she blushed becomingly and softly asked if it was true he'd had her, as a woman, on that wild night inside.

He said, ''I know you were only acting under orders of a

voodoo queen, and *my* excuse is that I was drunk as a skunk, ma'am.''

She demurely pointed out that neither of them was under any duress at the moment, the two of them were all alone out yonder, and he'd just saved her at least five thousand dollars.

He laughed and moved to mount his own paint as he lightly told her, ''That's a mighty tempting offer, ma'am. I don't reckon anyone's ever told you an arresting officer can have a tough time making his charge stick once he's had carnal knowlege of a lady suspect?''

She blushed, looked away, and asked him what on earth he meant to arrest her for.

To which he replied in good humor, ''Nothing, ma'am. Not as long as you say you only paid for a voodoo curse on the man who gunned your Tom. Proving you paid a hired assassin would be a bitch, even if I hadn't already been in you before you told me. I don't want you called as a material witness if it can be avoided. Seeing you don't seem to know where Queen Esther and her voodoo cult ran off to, I reckon it can be avoided now. So why don't I get you back to your library and we can quit whilst we're both ahead!''

That's what they did. When they got there she invited him inside for a minute, but he declined and rode back to his hotel, where he asked Calvin to saddle up a fresh mount for him while he ducked upstairs for a few minutes.

Once he had, he was glad Red Robin had left town as she'd warned him she might. For Felicidad lay spread-eagled and bare-assed across the bedcovers as he came in.

She waved lazily at the half-empty pitcher of sangria or ''bloodshed'' on the lamp table and remarked, ''What kept you? What's left is half water from the melted ice. Where have you been all this time?''

Longarm barred the door and hung up his hat as he honestly replied, ''Out to that old cotton spread your finance company still pays taxes on. You'd have a record if anybody had leased the property, say, to grow cotton or raise hell?''

Felicidad propped herself up on one elbow, shapely thighs

still spread in welcome, as she remarked in an uncaring tone, "You asked me aboard that train and while we were going through the files in the office, darling. Nobody ever told me a thing about any colored woman renting, squatting on, or just passing through that failed plantation. If you think our runner, Howard, was getting tips on bail-skippers from some colored mastermind, why don't you take it up with him?"

Longarm said, "I mean to. You said he was out to the Wedford home spread with Sam and the other recovery riders? I reckon I'd best take along some gunhands of my own. The Rangers will be hurt if they're left out. But I'd best invite some county law to ride with us, seeing some morals charges may be prosecuted by Dallas County."

She put her free hand to the part between her open thighs as she pouted, "Can't it wait until later in the day, when it's cooled off outside? I'm still hot *inside,* and you promised to fulfill me once you had me alone up here!"

Longarm moved over to the bedstead, but didn't unbuckle or unbutton anything as he sat down. He said, "I know what I said. I wanted you alone up here while I rode out to that plantation to see if I could catch you in two places at the same time again. By sheer luck I stumbled over a piece of the puzzle that fits others together just swell. My boss, Marshal Billy Vail, keeps hammering at us to make sure we can prove motive, means, and opportunity before we arrest anybody. The means and opportunity have been there to see all along. It was a sensible *motive* for all this razzle-dazzle I was searching for in vain."

She sat up to lay a languid hand on his thigh as she said she had no idea what he was talking about.

He snorted, "Hell, girl, you were working right there in the office. You typed up the very papers those hired killers used to justify all those expensive executions. A heap of lawmen aside from me saw right off that it made no sense to skip bail and go down fighting to avoid no more than a modest fine or a few days on a county road gang. The Caddo Kid told me early on that your outfit was getting tips from a network of half-invisible colored help, controlled by a spooky voodoo queen. I had no trouble making those pieces fit. You can't hardly keep a voodoo cult a serious secret if you want superstitious white folks to bring money.''

She moved her hand closer to his groin as she sighed and said she didn't want to talk about silly white housewives rutting with field hands at voodoo orgies. She said, ''Come on. Take off your clothes and fulfill me some more as a woman, darling!''

He calmly replied, ''I thought I already had, considerably. You've known all along who I was. You had your voodoo spies watching for me before I could get here. You set out to confound me at your *banda* the other night by changing costumes, or the lack of the same, more than once. You served me that doped drink as a naked white gal with your copper hair under black silk and that star hanging upside down betwixt those same swell tits. Then you slipped upstairs to interview me as a colored voodoo queen with every square inch of her skin covered, and then you had someone in your skull mask and fright wig grinning down at us whilst you and them other gals got fulfilled with me on the main floor. You headed me off this morning to fool me some more because, like another naughty gal I've been fulfilling, you heard an arresting officer finds it awkward in court when the accused can charge he took advantage of her before or after he arrested her.''

She tried to spring up from beside him. Longarm hauled her back down and placed her across his knees, warning, ''I'll spank you if you don't just hush and listen. Lord knows you have a good spanking coming. But it ain't too late to turn state's evidence and save your lawyers explaining all them voodoo sex orgies to a prim and proper jury of Southern Baptists.''

So in the end, that was what Queen Esther née Felicidad Torres and Longarm agreed might be best for the both of them.

# Chapter 21

Leaving the copper-haired gal fulfilled and worried sick, Longarm rode north along the west banks of the Trinity at the head of a much bigger posse than he'd planned. Since so many of the murders had been out of state, Longarm had federal jurisdiction. The Rangers wanted a slice of the pie because so many of the accused had been killed off in other parts of Texas. The Dallas Sheriff's Department took the not-unreasonable position that wherever they'd been killed, most of the victims had been slated for a hearing in a Dallas County court. That added up to thirty-seven determined riders, Longarm included, loaded for bear and spoiling for a fight.

As in most counties at the time, the local property taxes were collected by the Sheriff's Department. So Undersheriff Spitzer had more than one deputy under him who knew the way to the Wedford home spread Sam Wedford had told Felicidad he was headed to. It sat atop a rise overlooking the broad and muddy shallows of the river. There was a quarter mile of overgrazed open ground sloping down from the thick sod walls of the sprawl atop the rise. One of the county men allowed the place had been laid out back when the Comanche had still been mightly surly, and the Wedfords had bought the stronghold from its original owners in more recent times. The main house, stables, and storage sheds were wrapped around a central patio with a well and no easy way to get at their horses from outside.

The posse swung inland to circle just outside rifle range, and then dismount along the service road and ditch that cut across the sort of oxbowed rise the stronghold stood on.

Crack willow and alder had naturally sprung up along the roadside drainage ditch to offer some cover, although none of the greenery was bullet proof, like those thick sod walls atop the rise. The riders with Longarm dismounted to lead their ponies along the far side of the tanglewood, and tethered them to browse well spread out.

Then Undersheriff Spitzer said he knew some of the house servants personally, and nobody objected when he stepped through some alders to gingerly head up the slope, waving a white kerchief as he called out in a jovial tone, "Hello the spread up yonder! This would be Undersheriff Spitzer of the Dallas County Sheriff's Department, and I have to talk to you all about some gunplay near and far."

A familiar voice called down the slope, "That's far enough for now. I assume you have a warrant allowing you to set one fucking foot on private property this evening?"

Spitzer called back, "Is that you, Howard Brinks? As a paid-up member of the courthouse gang, you know it ain't going to do you a lick of good to pick legal nits with us. Can't I just come up alone and talk to you and Sam?"

There was a cotton puff of gun smoke from a small open window near a closed door facing them, followed by the whip-crack of a Winchester and that same voice yelling louder, "Next shot will be *aimed,* damn your eyes! You know the law and you're talking to a lawyer who knows the law even better!"

The Texas Ranger in command, a Sergeant Ledbetter, snorted, "Shit! Why don't we form a skirmish line and call their bluff? The late sun is low behind us and how many of us could they hope to stop, even if they have the balls?"

The dozen Rangers with him thought that sounded reasonable. But Undersheriff Spitzer called out to one of his own riders, "Farnsworth, ride back to the courthouse and tell Judge Culhane we need a warrant to serve on the silly bastards."

Turning to Longarm, he asked what the best charge might be.

Longarm said, "Criminal conspiracy ought to cover everything I can prove so far."

Spitzer moved back to cover with the rest of them as he told his own deputy, "You heard the man. What are you waiting for, a kiss good-bye?"

Farnsworth ran for his pony, bawling, "Hot damn! Conspired criminals! Ain't that a bitch?"

As the county rider mounted up to head back to town, the older and more weary-looking undersheriff told the Ranger sergeant, "I formed in with a skirmish line under General Hood at Chicky Magua one time. The Bluebellies shot us to pieces as we moved up the slope singing 'The Eyes of Texas' until they got our lead tenor. I don't lead skirmish lines up-slope across open fields of fire anymore. It won't take old Farnsworth more than an hour to get back with that warrant, and if it does take him longer, they ain't *going* nowheres, are they?"

Sergeant Ledbetter grimaced and said, "Not before dark they ain't."

Longarm chewed thoughtfully on an unlit cheroot as he peered through some crack willow at the sod walls glowing orange against a purple sky to the east and reluctantly declared, "The Ranger has a point, you know. If *I* was holed up atop that rise against these odds, I'd stall until after sundown and then try for a break down the bluffs to the river."

Undersheriff Spitzer called out, "Deputy Hammond, form a squad of eight and lead 'em around to cover the east side. You all might be able to work along the river's edge until you're right under anybody coming down that dirt bluff at you. Move it out and shoot to kill if they make a break for the water in the dark."

A couple of Rangers asked for and received permission to go along with the grimly smiling county riders. As they all worked their way south behind the screen of weed trees, Undersheriff Spitzer turned to Longarm to say, "I hope they'll listen to reason once I have some fool papers to wave at 'em. Lawyers are like that. If we have to kill old Sam and his sidekick Brinks, we'll never know just why they had all those men gunned under false pretense as bail-jumpers."

Longarm shook his head and said, "I thought you understood that part, sir. The voodoo queen they were working with was selling *wangas* or death curses against men some of her white followers wanted dead. Some were false-hearted lovers. Others had done somebody wrong. In any case, hardly any hired guns are simply going to blow away a man with no excuse at all. Not at a price Sam Wedford was willing to pay, leastways. The sort of gent who winds up with bitter women paying to have him cursed by the voodoo spirits tends to be a drifting soul who loves 'em and leaves 'em, or blows a young punk away in a whorehouse brawl and gets on out of town himself. So they were able to offer death curses on distant targets their voodoo pals had been keeping tabs on with the help of the invisible servants' grapevine. Once they had an execution planned, they'd simply send a ringer in to get picked up on a minor charge. Then they'd bail him out and he'd crawl back under his wet rock whilst the Caddo Kid, Lash Legrange, or whoever moved in, armed with papers to justify their actions to the local law, and just blow the unsuspecting target away."

He decided he might as well smoke the cheroot as chew it soggy, and proceeded to do so as he added, "Now and again some cuss like the late Charles Edward Taylor fought back. Most of them didn't. In either case, the superstitious and vengeful gals who'd paid to have the target *wanga*'d were satisfied and paid the balance on their *wanga* bill. If one such gal I questioned paid the going rate, the Triple 6 cum voodoo cult was asking ten thousand for a serving of such magical revenge."

Spitzer whistled and demanded, "Who's got that sort of money to spend on black magic? Ten thousand dollars is more than most workingmen are likely to earn in twenty years or more!''

Longarm dryly observed, ''It would take someone like a librarian or schoolmarm longer. But old Sam was willing to *finance* the black magic. The revenge-seeking gals didn't know he was in on it when they went to a finance company suggested by their helpful voodoo queen. They thought they were borrowing the money to pay for a voodoo curse. Sam lent it at high interest, accepting real estate as security. He got the money right back, from his voodoo confederates. Then he got the real estate when the desperate borrower naturally failed to pay back the loan. Like you just said, where in thunder could your average dabbler in the occult ever earn ten thousand dollars?''

The man who helped collect county taxes declared, ''We were wondering how Sam Wedford had accumulated all those odd bits and pieces of land he owns, scattered all across Dallas County. Nobody who used to own a vacant lot or a chicken farm is about to declare they gave 'em up to hoodoo-voodoo notions! But what might old Sam *want* with such a patchwork of small holdings? I can see how they didn't cost him half as much as he should have paid. But who would pay *anything* for such odd lots of land?''

Longarm said, ''Folks who want land in the growing Fort Worth-Dallas transportation and business center, of course. Thanks to the war, Reconstruction, and that depression of the early '70's, Texas got sort of left behind as the rest of the West started booming after the war. But with restored self-rule and the growing rail-net, things will pick up in these parts a heap ere long. Growing towns need land, and they don't make new land from thin air. So a vacant lot here and some truck or grazing land there will surely grow in value, year by year, as sly old Sam just bides his time like a spider in its web.''

Longarm had barely finished his cheroot when Deputy Farnsworth returned at a lope, waving the fresh warrant from town.

Sergeant Ledbetter warned it wasn't going to work. But to Longarm's and likely even Spitzer's surprise, the lawyer up in the Wedford home spread allowed the three of them to approach on foot and serve what the pragmatic Sergeant Ledbetter dismissed as a meaningless sheet of ass-wipe.

Then, standing in the doorway after reading it, the crablike Howard Brinks gravely said, "I deny any knowledge of any criminal conspiracy. You'll have to take this up with Sam Wedford, not me."

Longarm soberly allowed that was why they'd ridden out there. But Brinks just grinned like a shit-eating dog and replied, "He's not here. He sent word I was to meet him out here with some of the boys. But he hasn't shown up so far."

Sergeant Ledbetter roared, "You son of a bitch! You've been stalling us all this time and now I'm going to start busting your fingers, one by one, till you tell us where he's run off to!"

Longarm softly said, "Don't bust him up, Sarge. He'll play his bruises for sympathy in court, and I doubt he really knows. Wedford's flimflammed everyone else. Why wouldn't he flimflam his own? When he read about Lash Legrange's mistake in the morning papers, he sent his office gal to slow me down by telling me he was out here. I doubt she knew different. She said, and we see it's true, that he'd ordered this courthouse runner and the rest of his crew to hole up out here until further notice. That gave him the whole morning to play a lone hand in town without anybody on either side watching too close, see?"

They saw. They marched everyone out of the house and down the slope for a head count in the soft light of the gloaming. Longarm spotted a tall familiar figure dressed cow. It was the ringer they'd sent in to be picked up and bailed out as the late Slim Thorp. It was Brinks who protested they had horses and saddles back up the rise.

Undersheriff Spitzer smiled indulgently and said, "The walk back to town in this tricky light won't kill you. It'll make it easier for *us* to kill you if you make a break for it on foot.

168

You'll get to take off your boots and rest your weary asses all night, once we have you back to the county jail!''

Sergeant Ledbetter chuckled and said, ''Grand notion. Wrong destinattion, pard. These old boys are going to be tried by the State of Texas, and meanwhile, they're headed for our state holding cells at our own station house!''

Longarm didn't say anything about federal courts. He didn't really care, and it was up to the conflicting jurisdictions to decide, as long as *somebody* put the rascals away for some time at hard.

At the bottom of the rise they handcuffed the prisoners and ran a throw-rope through the resulting wrist loops to lead them afoot in a protesting line as all the lawmen got to ride.

Moving on out, Ledbetter suggested, ''We'd best put an all-points on the wire as soon as we get back to town. Wedford has had almost a full day to run. But Texas is a considerable state and we're close to the center of it. So how far could he have gotten? Couple of hundred miles by rail at the most?''

Undersheriff Spitzer objected, ''A man running that serious stands out on the mostly empty range all around. And I doubt he could be running light. It must hurt enough to abandon all the odd lots of land he's racked up with his hoodoo-voodoo shit. He'd never leave his hard cash behind, and a man running a finance company would have a lot of hard cash on hand to carry.''

Longarm said, ''I've heard there are Wedfords all over the county in town and country. But that sounds a tad obvious.''

The man who helped collect local taxes snorted, ''Suicidal is the word you're groping for, old son. Sam Wedford's two brothers fell for Texas in the war. Sam sat it out, buying cheap and selling dear. He has a sister who married up with another fighting Texican and hasn't spoken to Sam since. His other kin have little more use for old Sam. As these prisoners may have noticed by now, Sam Wedford looks out for himself and himself alone.''

Longarm said he'd heard another Wedford had a business in town. The man who knew the town better said, ''Sam's sissy cousin, Elroy. Sips tea with the ladies and sells them fancy books on flower arranging, female complaints, and such.''

Longarm grimaced and asked, "How about books on the occult? Spirit-rappings, fortune-telling, and such?"

Spitzer shrugged and replied, "How should I know? We only collect property taxes off Elroy Wedford. You never see no grown men hanging around his prissy bookshop on Latimer Street.''

Longarm rode on thoughtfully before he asked, "Can anyone tell me how long any Wedfords have used that 666 brand?''

Spitzer said, "Sure. I can. They've used it since old Pop Wedford came out here from Dixie with his darkies and cotton seed to discover he could make money easier and faster with cows. Captain Ewen Cameron had just brung the first longhorns up from Mexico. Some Mexicans were sore as hell about that too. That 666 was the trail brand of a herd Pop Wedford bought off another enterprising Texican as a spoil of war. I know what some say about the number of the Beast. Them Mexican beasts were numbered 666. You'd have to ask the original Mexican owner why.''

Longarm nodded and said, "Could have been in memory of an old army unit, a street address, or hell, El Diablo himself. The point is that nobody in Sam Wedford's generation chose that particular number. They just inherited it, like the name Percy. Have you ever noticed that if you name a boy Bob, Bill, or Joe, he tends to just grow up, whilst do you name a boy Percy, he tends to grow up a sissy or a fighting fool?''

Sergeant Ledbetter asked what all this stuff about names and numbers had to do with the present whereabouts of the sinister Sam Wedford.

To which Longarm softly replied, "Maybe nothing. Maybe a lot. I'm more certain where he'd hiding out now. So with your permission I'll ride on alone and see what I can get out of him in private, man to man.''

# Chapter 22

Longarm got a full confession, once he'd convinced a thoroughly shaken Sam Wedford that he wasn't so smart, that his federal trial would take longer, and that full-time federal hangmen tended to make it short and snappy.

So nine days later Longarm was in the Denver chambers of Judge Dickerson, sipping Maryland rye with branch water and smoking one of those mild Cuban claros Judge Dickerson favored while His Honor puffed a mighty aromatic two-for-a-quarter and perused the modest official report Longarm had turned in.

Judge Dickerson peered through the blue haze with one bushy brow cocked as he told Longarm, "You sure like to keep all your sentences short and simple, you laconic young squirt. I'm not interested in any slap-and-tickle with these ladies you met along the way, but how the hell did you know where the ringleader, Sam Wedford, would be hiding out in the end?"

Longarm sipped from his tumbler, blew some smoke back at the judge, and replied, "There wasn't exactly one ringleader or one master plan, Your Honor. Things just brewed up mean and mysterious once at least three natural sneaks put their heads together to sort of surprise us all. Sort of like the way those old-time alchemists messed around until one day they mixed brimstone, charcoal, and cesspool salts to get one hell of an explosion.''

He took another well-earned sip and explained. ''Their evil plots just grew, like Topsy, to where there seemed to be a more clever one than there was. Stage magicians razzle-dazzle the audience that way. They get us to look everywhere but the right way as we try to catch 'em at something more clever. I understand professional magicians try not to perform before young kids because kids don't pay attention to the patter and tend to let their little eyes wander.''

He smiled sheepishly and confessed, ''I wasn't as good at catching the sleight of hand as your average four-year-old. I had to stumble over some of the pattern and have other parts explained to me before I had a clear picture of the whole picture. But naturally, once I was on to the way their devious minds had been working, it was simple to figure what any of 'em might try next.''

Judge Dickerson marveled, ''I'll be switched if I can see how you knew where Sam Wedford would go to ground once he'd lured all of you out to his 666 spread north of town. According to your own report here, he'd lied to both his court-house runner, Howard Brinks, and a voodoo queen he had on his payroll as a *typist*?''

As if that had been her cue, Miss Bubbles from the stenographers' pool came in, favoring Longarm with a shy, innocent smile as she handed the judge a Western Union telegram and asked if there was anything else she could do for them.

When neither man offered a decent or indecent proposal, the bubbly blonde left and Judge Dickerson tore open the telegram to scan it and gloat. ''The Texas Rangers just picked up Felicidad Torres, also known as Queen Esther. Did you know it was against the law to stage drunken sex orgies and blackmail crazy old white ladies by threatening to expose them to miscegenation charges?''

Longarm smiled thinly and said, ''I figured it might be, Your Honor. I got that suspect to come clean by offering not to press any *federal* charges. I figured all that stuff about rum-

172

and-coca love potions and odd religious notions might gum the works at a federal murder trial.''

''So you *did* screw her.'' Judge Dickerson sighed.

It had been a statement rather than a question, but Longarm chose to answer. ''Felicidad Torres was a French-Spanish Creole gal from the bayou country around New Orleans. Her quality family sent her to a convent school, but she wound up more interested in Satanism, black magic, or the less vicious African notions of some older house servants. She blew into Dallas after some scandal involving the jewelry and husbandry of other New Orleans belles. She got a job in a Dallas bookstore owned by one of Sam Wedford's less murderous relatives. They sold occult books on the art of turning frogs into princes or spinning gold from straw. A heap of bored and silly older women seem greatly interested in such shit. So to make a long story short, our Felicidad was soon running a voodoo cult that accepted white members, for a nominal fee.''

Judge Dickerson asked, ''How does a white convent gal get to be a voodoo queen, for Pete's sake?''

Longarm shrugged and said, ''Same way the white Simon Girty or the half-white Quanah Parker got to lead Indian war bands, I reckon. When someone with more education, more pocket jingle, and a better understanding of the way this white world works volunteers to be the leader, your average medicine man or voodoo *hungan* hasn't got much to sell in the way of a counter-offer. As Queen Esther, made up to look more like a haunt than black or white, Felicidad soon had her colored followers laughing like hell while they took advantage in every way of confused and superstitious white folks. I suspect some of the white *men* rolling around on the floor out at that voodoo *humfo* were just using religion as an excuse to fuck young gals. Lord knows you see a lot of that at Sunday-Go-to-Meetings-on-the-Green. But what was going on was going on until Sam Wedford's courthouse runner, Howard Brinks, started coming to her *banda* rites to change his luck and nose around on the seamy side of Big D.''

Judge Dickerson asked, ''Then did they corrupt Queen Esther, or did she turn that bail-bonding company into an assassination society?"

Longarm shrugged and asked, "Did that alchemist drop the brimstone into the saltpeter or was it the other way around? Before they met up with Felicidad, Sam Wedford and his crew ran that Triple 6 as a hard-nosed cut-and-dried bail-bonding operation, as part of old Sam's moneylending and realty interests. As you first pointed out to me in these very chambers a spell back, there'd be little call for a cut-and-dried bail bondsman to kill many clients. Until he met up with Queen Esther, Howard Brinks just didn't offer to go to the bail of anyone he considered a poor risk. Lash Legrange alone was enough to deal with the few troublesome cases."

The judge asked, "Then Felicidad Torres, as Queen Esther, was the one who who came up with the mass-murder schemes you let her off on?"

Longarm said reassuringly, "She'll really look like an old witch by the time they let her out, and she swore that the more murderous notions just grew, like Topsy."

He drained his tumbler and set it empty on the judge's desk as he went on. "She said all she was up to at first was fingering a few bail-jumpers in the habit of hanging around colored whorehouses or screwing religiously at voodoo ceremonies. She couldn't offer much help with owlhoot riders who frequented *Mexican* pool halls or slept with Caddo gals. But she was able to finger a good many, and moved to the Triple 6 office as a white typewriter-player to hide her true identity and account for her nice clothes and fashionable quarters, apart from her voodoo pals. She naturally kept in touch with the country-wide net of voodoo folks and so she was a wonder at tracking down lowlifes who spent more time in colored quarters across the land."

Judge Dickerson asked, "When did the killings start?"

Longarm said, "As soon as a bitter white lady who dabbled in the occult came to Queen Esther for a *wanga* she was willing to pay a lot for."

He placed a palm over his empty tumbler to politely but

silently refuse another shot as he continued. "The man who'd done the old bat wrong had naturally been humping her at voodoo gatherings. So Queen Esther knew who he was and where he'd run off to with the fat old white gal's jewelry. But when she asked Lash Legrange if he wanted to *wanga* the false-hearted-lover with his .50-50, Lash demured that he was only allowed to gun bail-jumpers."

Judge Dickerson grimaced and said, "Your report explains how they sent in ringers to be arrested on petty charges and released on bail-bonding contracts that amounted to death warrants. You say ten grand was the going price for such voodoo curses? That'a a heap of money!"

Longarm shrugged and said, "Nobody asks a voodoo queen to cast a death spell unless they're really in the market for one. They took five thousand in advance and five thousand after the voodoo victim's name appeared in the obituary columns. They didn't have to worry about any customers holding out on that last payment. Would you hold back the rent on a landlord who could have you death-cursed instead of evicted?"

Judge Dickerson shook his head and said, "All right. You've covered all that clear enough. As a combined voodoo queen and finance-office typist, Felicidad Torres was helping them peddle curses and loan money to pay for them, with real estate as the security. Legrange and that other killer, the Caddo Kid, made good on the cursed mammy men after their sneaky courthouse runner, Brinks, convinced the innocent but overworked court clerks they were out on bail, right?"

Longarm nodded soberly and said, "Recruiting Cahill, the Caddo Kid, was a mistake. But it was getting too busy for old Lash. The self-styled Caddo Kid wasn't half as smart. But he was crazy mean. We might not have noticed if Lash Legrange had just come up here to Denver and blown that Gaston Dumas away on a bail-jumping charge."

Judge Dickerson nodded and said, "I still don't understand them dragging *you* into their beeswax with all that gunplay over on Tremont Place."

Longarm explained, "That was a clumsy attempt to kill a flock of birds with one stone. Gaston Dumas knew as much or more about voodoo as they did. He'd somehow discovered they were after him, not for that staged kitchen cutting, but because hell had no fury like an old white lady who'd caught him changing his luck with her younger and somewhat darker upstairs maid. Dumas got his own voodoo pals to throw Queen Esther's voodoo pals off his trail. So Cahill, knowing nobody at all in the Denver quarter, wanted to enlist my help in getting him into Madame Pickles' place."

"By shooting you in the back?" marveled the older man.

Longarm explained. "Texas Bob White was a half-ass gunslick who'd had no luck hiring out his gun of late. He and the Caddo Kid went back to time served together on a Texas chain gang. He had no idea what an old pal was doing for the Triple 6, but he wanted in on it and refused to back off as he dogged a more serious hired gun. So once they were here in Denver, the Caddo Kid convinced Texas Bob I was the target, and the two of them waited in front of the Overland Terminal to kill me on my way to work that morning."

Judge Dickerson said, "Say no more. I see it all. The Caddo Kid was out to make friends with you by backshooting a pal he'd asked to backshoot you!"

Longarm shrugged and dryly observed, "The man who first coined the notion of honor among thieves must not have known many thieves. After Cahill convinced me I was in his debt, he used me as a guide to Madame Pickles and a semi-witness to his cold-blooded execution of Gaston Dumas, guilty of no more than an enormous and unwise indulgence in the pursuit of pussy."

He shook his head wearily and continued. "He should have quit while he was ahead. His luck ran out in Dodge when tried to pull the same shit on another white cocksman sleeping with another voodoo queen or tea-leaf reader. We know how his run-in with the late Charles Edward Taylor turned out. By pure shithouse luck I tangled with a similar sort of situation when you sent me over to Dodge. Another gal entirely with no voodoo connections bought our story about me being a hired gun, and when she tried to hire me, the bully she wanted gunned, the late Simon Fuller, came gunning for me and made our story about Cross Culpepper sound even better.''

Judge Dickerson said, "Yet Lash Legrange never trusted you, even though he was there when you had to gun Simon Fuller?"

Longarm shrugged and decided, "He might have just been jealous. Old Felicidad confessed she'd been trying to trick me into confiding my true identity because she couldn't trace any Cross Culpepper far enough back. Catching up with Big Thumb Gatewood with the papers the real bounty hunter would have had on him helped a lot. But even after I was working for them and caught Lash red-handed, I was still confused until a library gal who'd paid to have her son's killer killed dropped the last piece of the puzzle in place for me.''

"What was this librarian like in bed?" asked the judge, knowingly.

Longarm truthfully replied, "I never had her in no bed, and weren't you asking how I knew where to look for Sam Wedford after he'd run off with the money and left his followers holding the bag?''

The judge grinned like a mean little kid and said, "I wish I could have been there! He must have shit when he saw *you* standing there!''

Longarm replied, "He'd already shit in public, dressed in old clothes with no visible means, to have himself thrown in jail that morning as Felicidad was sent to head me off and steer me towards his home spread. I knew he'd have had to cache all that money he was packing and hole up close to it. I knew he knew we'd know all the usual hiding places in or around Dallas. So I just looked for him in the one place he figured no lawman might look. And there he was, in the county jail, and come to study on it, he did look as if he might be shitting in his pants when he saw he couldn't stay there until his trail cooled off.''

The judge laughed again, and didn't seem to mind when

Longarm got to his feet, mildly observing it was after quitting time.

The judge allowed he'd done well, and offered him another shot of the good stuff before he went saloon-crawling on Larimer Street. But then the tall deputy said he was meeting someone with delicate feelings about strong liquor that evening. So they shook on it, and Longarm was free to go at last.

But as he headed along the marble corridor amid the early bustle of quitting time, young Henry, from Billy Vail's office down the way, headed him off to say, "I hope you weren't planning on supper with that busty brunette who sells ladies hats?"

Longarm smiled at the typewriter-player and replied, "You must have been taking mind-reading lessons, Henry. What's it to you? You ain't been sparking Miss Billie whilst I've been out of town, have you?"

Henry blanched and said, "Heaven forfend! The guilty party is the hardware store owner down the street from her hat shop. I don't have a nicer way to put it, Custis, but—"

"There ain't no nicer way to put it," Longarm cut in, still smiling as he added, "I thank you for saving me from one of them drawing-room-comedy scenes you have to be a woman or an English dude to enjoy worth mention."

Henry said, "I'm glad you've taken it so well. What other plans do you have for this evening? There's a new vaudeville bill over to the Apollo Hall if you'd care to take it in with me."

Longarm replied firmly but not unkindly, "No offense, Henry, but you just ain't my type. Why don't you make the same offer down the hall in the stenographers' pool before they all get away this evening?"

Then he left, still smiling, to grab a bowl of chili con carne up on Broadway and forge on up Capitol Hill, feeling fortified.

Ready for anything, he twisted the doorbell of a certain plush brownstone on tree-shaded Sherman Street. A million years went by and then, just as he was about to turn away, a

shapely bare arm reached out to grab him by one sleeve and haul him inside.

The voluptuous widow woman with the light brown hair had light brown hair all over, as one could see by the gloaming light through her vestibule door's frosted glass. She'd thrown her kimono to the hall rug to hug him and sob, "Oh, Custis. I was so afraid my foolish jealousy had driven you from me forever!"

He got a good grip on her bare curves to kiss her back before he calmly asked, "What were you so jealous about this time?"

She laughed through her tears and said, "Someone told me you'd been messing with that Miss Bubbles at the Federal Building. That's why I was so cruel to you the other night. I'd no sooner slammed that very door in your face before another friend told me Miss Bubbles has been keeping company with your friend, Deputy Smiley. Can you forgive a poor silly for thinking you'd been sparking another girl behind her back?"

To which he gallantly replied, "I reckon. But you should be ashamed of yourself for suspecting me of messing with any other gals here in Denver. You're the only Denver gal I've been this close to in recent memory." And that was the simple truth, as soon as one studied on it.

Watch For

**LONGARM AND THE LADY FROM
TOMBSTONE**

247<sup>th</sup> novel in the exciting LONGARM series
from Jove

*Coming in July!*

**Explore the exciting Old West with one of the men who made it wild!**

# JAKE LOGAN

## TODAY'S HOTTEST ACTION WESTERN!